As Long as You Stay Down

by

K.L. HALL

This book is a work of fiction. Names, characters, places and incidents are either the product of the author's imagination or are used fictionally. Any resemblance to actual persons, living or dead, or to actual events or locales is entirely coincidental.

Imprint: K.L. Hall Productions, LLC.
ISBN: 978-1-7366663-0-2

Synopsis

It's the time of year when family is cherished, gifts are exchanged, and memories are made. Yet, when a snowstorm grounds all outgoing flights, Aris finds herself confined within the four walls of her apartment for the holidays. In an attempt to savor the last ounce of holiday spirit she has left, she decides to order in and submerge herself in a holiday movie marathon.

A simple knock on her door sets the rest of her night in motion when she finds herself face to face with a handsome delivery driver. Moving off vibes and impulse alone, she invites him in from the cold. As the night unfolds, the chemistry between them becomes powerful enough to devour them whole, but the secret he's hiding could easily extinguish the flames.

She soon learns that their encounter wasn't by chance. In fact, she's the only thing standing in between him and the one thing he's been waiting seven years to reconnect with. When the truth is disclosed, he offers her something that could change the course of her mundane life forever. But at what cost? In the end, the cold winter wind just may blow her down a path she doesn't want to go, but escaping just may not be so easy.

This is a novella. If you don't enjoy short stories, please choose another full-length article from my catalog.

Epigraph

"You're my heaven; you're my hell.
You're my now; you're my forever.
You're my freedom; you're my jail."

-Kanye West

*****

It was the time of year when the days were shorter and the nights grew longer. The holiday season had made its way around once more, filling the city with bright twinkling lights and warm Christmas melodies blaring within a three-mile radius of the next. Yet, an irritated Aris found herself lugging her two-ton suitcase down the hallway to her apartment door with her phone pressed against her ear.

"I know tomorrow is Christmas Eve, but there aren't any more available flights?" she asked.

"For the fourth time, ma'am, no, there aren't any flights going out right now due to the snowstorm," the airline customer service rep told her.

"Can you please just check again? Have a heart; it's almost Christmas!" she pleaded.

He snorted. "I don't celebrate Christmas; I'm a Jehovah's Witness."

She rolled her eyes. "Whatever. Thanks for nothing," she said and hung up.

The heat roared in the background as she pushed the door open and tossed her jingling keys and purse on the table beside her front door. She slid off her snow-dusted Ugg Boots and sighed. Aggravated wasn't the word. Aris was pissed. All modes of transportation had been canceled due to the endless snowfall outside her window. She had to face the fact that she'd be spending Christmas alone. As a mental health case manager, she knew the holidays could take a toll on one's mental health. She'd saved up enough PTO to take off an entire week and was looking forward to heading home for the holidays to see her family. Her hometown right outside of Boston was only an hour flight and a five-hour drive, but the roads were practically already covered with sheets of snow.

She glanced over at her suitcase resting by the door, mentally not in the mood to unpack a damn thing. "Well, if I can't go to Christmas, I'll just roll one and celebrate the holidays here," she said while heading to the bathroom to roll herself a fresh blunt.

There was something about the metaphysical state marijuana put her mind in that made her fall in love with being high in her early twenties. Now in the latter years of her twenties, she'd become a functioning pothead. As her job demands became more and more prevalent, the more she felt the need to smoke to cope with the day. Being high just seemed to be the only thing that took the edge off, if only for the moment.

The shower pumped out warm water, causing the bathroom mirror to fog up as she sat naked on the toilet seat, rolling her blunt. Smoke danced freely in the air as she exhaled, waving all of the excess smoke out of the small square window by the shower. Once she'd showered off the airport stench and changed into her PJs, she peeked through her blinds. Crystals of snow were still falling steadily, slowly burying all the parked cars as the wind blew tiny flakes against the window. She scooped up her phone and headed into the kitchen to make her favorite Christmas concoction. One part eggnog, two parts Hennessy, a tablespoon of brown sugar, and a single teaspoon of nutmeg and cinnamon.

Aris took a sip and smiled before plugging in the tabletop Christmas tree wrapped in tinsel and decorated with mini ornaments. It didn't do much to help illuminate her one-bedroom apartment, but it was the thought that counted. She could already feel the Christmas spirit beginning to pump through her veins. Her phone vibrated right after she took a large swig from her mug. Her eyes lit up with excitement, followed by a stiff frown. She was not in the mood to tell her mother about the last four and a half hours she'd spent in the airport only to end up back at home. *"At least having the conversation while buzzed will make it easier,"* she thought to herself. Aris knew her parents would curl up and die if they knew she'd been smoking the "devil's grass," as they called it. They'd always raised her to be on the straight and narrow, and the older she got, the more she found herself straying away from her sheltered upbringing.

"Ugh, fuck," she mumbled before pressing accept. "Hey, Mama!"

"The fact that you answered the phone lets me know that you're not going to make it home for Christmas."

Aris's head did a quick bobble. "Yeah, everything is canceled. Nothing is coming in or going out until this freakish storm is over," she said, breaking the news.

"Oh, I'm so sorry. We were all looking forward to seeing you. It has been way too long."

She sucked her teeth. "I know. I was looking forward to seeing everyone too. Tell Des and Kiara I got the card and the cute pictures of the kids. They are getting so big now!"

"They looked so cute in their matching Christmas PJs, didn't they?" Her mother agreed.

"Yeah, they did. How's Daddy doing?"

"You know your father, always busy trying to take care of everything and everybody, just like you."

She nodded. "I guess I have it honest."

"You sure do. When do you go back to work?"

"I have a whole week off. Hopefully, this snow doesn't keep me trapped in the house the entire time."

"Do you have enough food stashed? What about batteries for your flashlight and candles just in case the power goes out?" Her mother probed.

Aris smiled a lopsided grin. She had batteries; they just weren't in her flashlight. "Yeah, I'll be good, Mama. I'm about to see if I can get a delivery order in real quick before everything in the whole city shuts down."

The last thing she wanted to do was be stuck at home in the middle of a snowstorm with the munchies.

"Okay, well, make sure your phone is charged and that you've got enough blankets just in case. I'll call you tomorrow, okay?"

Aris appreciated that her mother's level of concern hadn't changed, although the number of miles that separated them was plentiful. "Okay, Mama. I love you."

"I love you, too. Try and relax, okay? You deserve a break."

"I will, Mama. I'll talk to you soon."

She ended the call and walked over to the couch while pulling up her favorite restaurant on DoorDash to place a quick order. If she couldn't spend Christmas with her family, at least she could stuff her face with food while baking Snickerdoodles and immersing herself in every Christmas movie the Hallmark channel had to offer. She smiled as soon as she was notified the restaurant confirmed her order. Aris wasted no time facing the remainder of her blunt and pressing play on the holiday playlist she'd initially curated for her family before putting the first batch of cookies into the oven. She was determined to turn her apartment into a mini Christmas miracle while she waited on her dinner.

"Oh, the weather outside is frightful, but the fire is so delightful. And since we've no place to go, let it snow, let it snow, let it snow."

Once the cookies were in the oven, she snuggled up on the couch underneath her plush throw blanket. Her mother was right; she needed the break. Her job was taxing, to say the least. She could honestly say it wasn't what she thought it would be when she first started. Day in and day out, she poured herself into her work, trying to ensure her clients were as mentally stable as they could be when it came time for them to reenter the real world. Yet, it seemed like most of them couldn't care less. Aris had spent most of her life taking care of others, it wasn't as if it was something she didn't enjoy, but it would've been nice to be on the receiving end once in a while. Those thoughts made her question if she was she was pleased with the life she was living. There was no doubt that she needed something to take her life in a spontaneous new direction, but she wasn't in the right position financially to find a new job. Relaxation was at the top of her Christmas list, but it wasn't *all* she needed. She knew beggars couldn't be choosy, but she wouldn't complain if Santa tossed some good wood her way for Christmas. She'd done more than her share of good deeds that year.

*****

FORTY MINUTES LATER, she heard a knock on her door. Knowing it was her food, she skipped over and swung it open. To her surprise, her eyes zeroed in on a man standing there with her food in hand.

"I got a delivery for, uh, somebody named Aris," he said, staring at the receipt stapled to the bag with her name on it.

Her eyebrows knitted. She wanted to yell, but her mouth was just too dry to let a word slip off her tongue. "Knock and go," she mumbled.

"What?"

"Those were the instructions I put in the app. You were just supposed to knock, drop the food at my door and go," she said, folding her arms across her chest.

He stared at her blankly while chewing the inside of his lip. "Oh, uh. My fault," he said, taking a few steps back.

Aris's eyes rolled. "Whatever, just put it down, and I'll grab it."

Him standing in front of her wasn't going to increase the tip she'd already given him. She watched him put her bagged dinner at her feet and step back. He didn't look like what she expected him to. Not that anyone named *Mohammad* had to look a certain way, but she was presently surprised. The first things she noticed were the multiple tattoos he had on his honey-brown face. There were names written in script on each temple, a Chinese symbol beside his left eye, and a cross in his right ear. His six-foot-five stature easily towered over Aris's five-foot-five frame, making her feel tiny. His athletic build made it easy to see he had muscles even through the bulkiness of his winter coat. His full beard, mustache, and goatee made him a triple threat. The only things she wasn't too fond of were the six straight back medium-sized cornrows he was rockin' as if it was 2002.

"Thank you," she said in a softer tone.

His head tipped forward in a nod. "No problem..."

As easy as it should've been for her to turn and shut the door in his face, give him a 2-star rating and return to her Christmas vibe, it wasn't. "It's uh, really coming down out there, huh?" she asked, noticing the globs of snow that hadn't managed to melt off his Timberland boots.

"Yeah, it is…"

Silence hung in between them like popcorn on a string. One thing Aris hated was the fact that she could easily read people. It wasn't hard for her to tell that his minimal holiday spirit was broken entirely just by looking in his dark brown eyes.

"Yo, is somethin' burnin'?" He asked, darting his eyes past her.

"Oh shit, the cookies!" She yelled, dropping her dinner and running back into the kitchen.

Mohammad watched her toss the cookie sheet with crispy, burnt lumps on it onto the stovetop. She was waving her potholders in the air to try and prevent the smoke detector from going off. He bent down to pick up her food, making sure not to step over the threshold into her actual apartment. Once Aris was able to get the smoke cleared, she looked back at the doorway and saw him still standing there like an obedient dog. As much as things hadn't seemed to be going her way, she was suddenly filled to the brim with holiday cheer.

"Uh, do you want to come in for coffee or some hot chocolate to warm up for a bit? I know you basically risked your life coming out here in this weather."

"Yeah, uh, thank you," he said, stepping inside and taking in his surroundings. He drew in a deep breath, inhaling the burnt cookies' smell comingled with the marijuana aroma in the air.

"You can just put the food over on the counter after you take off your shoes," she said, eyeing his boots once more.

When his shoes were off and the food was on the counter, Mohammad slid off his jacket and the hoodie underneath. Aris quickly clenched her thighs together at the sight of him. The simple white tee he was wearing fit as if it had been tailor-made for his body. His muscles bulged in all the right places. She gazed at the print of his puffed chest and washboard abs hiding beneath the layer of clothing closest to his body. Aside from the large rose tattooed on his throat, Mohammad had more tattoos drizzled down both arms, so much that Aris could only imagine where else ink resided on his chiseled body.

“So uh, coffee or hot chocolate?” she asked, snapping herself out of the daze he’d put her in. “I uh, I would offer you a cookie or two, but you see how that turned out.” She chuckled.

“Shit, they still might be edible,” he told her.

Aris eyed him closely as he made his way into her space and picked up one of the severely burnt cookies off the tray. It crumbled within seconds, snapping loudly with every bite.

“You don’t have to try and make me feel better by doing that,” she assured him.

“I’m not,” he told her, “and when you make the hot chocolate, I’ma dip another one in there, and the shit is gon’ be lit, trust me.”

“I’ll take your word for it,” she said, grabbing the hot chocolate K-cups from the cabinet.

“What’s that for?” he asked.

“What? These?” She asked, pointing to the K-cups in her hand.

“Yeah.”

“This is how you make hot chocolate. Well, the Keurig does it, for the most part, I just put it in there.” She laughed.

"Nah, that's not how you do it at all."
Aris scrunched her nose and arched a questioning eyebrow in his direction. "Excuse me?"

"I'm sayin' that's not how you make real hot chocolate."

"And how exactly do you like *your* hot chocolate?" she quizzed, unapologetically letting her attitude ring through her tone.

"If you got what I need, I'll show you because that shit ain't it," he said, pointing to the K-cups clutched in her hand.

"What do you need?"

"First off, I need milk. You don't make real hot chocolate with water."

"I have milk; what else?" She asked, folding her arms across her chest.

"Cocoa powder, sugar, a pot, and some chocolate chips if you got 'em."

As annoyed as she was that a stranger was trying to school her on making "real" hot chocolate, a part of her was intrigued. She was curious to see what he had up his sleeve. "I think I may have all of those things. Hold up and let me check."

Mohammad leaned against her kitchen counter while Aris started pulling out the ingredients he'd requested one by one. Once she'd placed everything on the counter in front of him, she stood back to watch him work his magic. He started by pouring the milk in the saucepan and turning on the burner closest to him. Next, he stirred in the cocoa powder and sugar. Once everything was warm, he poured in a handful of chocolate chips and stirred them into the pot until they melted into the mix.

"Taste it," he said, handing her a steaming mug.

She hesitantly reached out and grabbed the mug, eyeing him with suspicion before taking a sip. It was like heaven on her lips. It was the sweetest, creamiest thing she'd ever had in her life. Aris wasn't sure if it was as good as she thought it was or if she was just high. Regardless, she'd found home and peace of mind in a mug of homemade hot chocolate. "Wow…just wow," she said with her eyes closed.

"Shit is fire, right?" he asked.

Her mouth twisted into a smirk. "It's amazing. It's perfection in a fuckin' cup!"

"Told you. The secret is in the chocolate chips. Makes that shit extra chocolatey and creamy."

"I can honestly say this is the first time I think I've ever had homemade hot chocolate."

His head dipped in a quick nod. "Yeah, I ain't had this shit in years…since I was a kid and shit."

Aris shot him a sympathetic smile and quickly changed the subject. "This has to be one of the coldest freakin' days in history, if not *THE* coldest."

Mohammad bobbed his head in agreeance. "Hell yeah, it's cold as fuck outside."

"You know, it might not look like it in here, but Christmas is usually my favorite time of the year because it's the only time I get to see my family, but that weather outside is crazy."

"The whole city is shuttin' down."

"Yeah, I know. I should've checked the weather sooner. I don't know who I thought I was thinkin' I'd be able to hop on a plane and head home this close to Christmas, but as I said, the holidays are the only time I see my family."

"And why is that?" he asked, grabbing another burnt cookie off the sheet and dipping it into his mug.

"My job is pretty demanding."

"Word? What do you do?"

"Uh, I'm a case manager," she said, keeping it short. Every time she told someone what she did, she could tell they were either immediately bored to death or felt bad for her. He'd already witnessed her high ass burning cookies and schooled her on how to make hot chocolate. She didn't need any more sympathetic looks from him for the night.

"Yo, your food is probably cold as ice right now," he reminded her.

"You know, for some reason, I'm not as hungry as I was before. Plus, I wouldn't feel right eating in front of you."

"Nah, do your thing. I'm good with what I got right here," he said, dipping another cookie into his mug.

"Okay, cool. Well, feel free to chill in the living room. I'll be in there in a second."

*****

ARIS WALKED INTO the living room with her reheated dinner in hand and sat her food down in front of the couch. "Shit, I forgot to grab the fork. I'm gonna get another cup of hot chocolate while I'm in the kitchen. You want a refill too?"

"Yeah, this time spike mine with something strong. Don't act like I ain't see that bottle of Henny you got sittin' over here," Mohammad told her.

She smiled. "Coming right up."

Aris grabbed her phone off the coffee table and took it in to the kitchen before spiking their mugs of hot chocolate with a shot of Henny. Her eyes diverted to the cookie sheet, and she giggled. He'd eaten half of the blackened Snickerdoodles as if they were made just the way he liked them.

"What you in there smilin' about?" he asked.

She looked up and saw him staring back at her. The way his eyes hung onto hers as he spoke was enough to make her palms rain wet. "It's nothin'."

"People don't smile for nothin' unless they crazy," he told her.

Aris chuckled. "Nah, I just like to smile, and I like to make other people smile. But if you must know, I'm smiling because you demolished half of these burnt ass cookies."

He laughed. "I told you they were fine to me."

"Well, you are welcomed to the rest of them," she said, sneaking a peek out of the kitchen window. The snow had completely covered every square inch of the ground for as far as she could see. "Hey, is that your car?" she asked, pointing to the running car with the windshield wipers going on full blast and headlights barely shining underneath the pile of snow on the hood.

Mohammad walked over and eyed the car she was pointing to. "Nah, that's not mine."

"Oh, okay. I bet you can barely see where you parked with all this snow. And I'm sorry if I'm holding you up from delivering other orders, although I don't know how you'd do that in this weather."

"Nah, you were my last stop," he assured her.

"Oh, okay, good."

Before Mohammad could respond, Aris's phone began to ring. She reached out and picked up for her co-worker and friend, Yara.

"Hey Ya, what's up?" she answered.

"Girl! Please tell me you were able to get out of the city before this storm really kicked off."

Aris sucked her teeth. "Nope, no such luck. I'm back at my place, most likely snowed in for Christmas."

"As much as that sucks, I know you're happy you're not here, especially with everything that's going on!"

Aris's perfectly arched eyebrows creased. "What do you mean? What's going on?"

"You haven't seen the news?"

"No. What happened?"

"Oh my God, girl! We're under a whole fuckin' lockdown! Three inmates escaped from the fifth ward early this morning! Two guards are dead and everything. They aren't letting anyone in or out."

"Oh shit, are you fuckin' serious? Do you know who they were?"

Yara groaned. "The police are withholding that information right now. They are only referring to them by their inmate numbers."

"Wow, this is crazy."

"Crazy as fuck! You know, me being me, I tried to look that shit up, but I don't even have the right credentials to see that shit. I swear this is going to be the worst fuckin' Christmas ever."

Aris shook her head. She'd only heard stories about the fifth ward but had never once stepped foot on that floor in her seven and a half months of working at the prison. All she knew was it was the floor that housed the majority of the high profile criminals. She only worked with lower-level offenders who were a year or less away from their potential release dates. "Damn, well, just hang in there girl, and be careful."

"I'm safe in here; you be careful out there."

Aris rolled her eyes at how anxious Yara could be. "Don't worry about me. Nobody is going to bother me, especially not with the way this snow is coming down."

"Yeah, you're probably right about that."

"Just hang in there, okay? And keep me posted. I'll call you tomorrow."

"Um, why you trying to rush me off the phone? You got company or somethin'?" Yara quizzed.

"Mind your business and Merry Christmas!" Aris told her friend before ending the call.

“Everything good?” Mohammad queried.

“Yeah, I’m fine. Just work stuff,” she said, shrugging it off as if it was nothing.

“You said you a case manager and shit? You work with foster kids or somethin’?”

Aris massaged the back of her neck. “No, I uh. I work with adults, but can we not talk about my job right now? I’m trying this whole thing where I’m trying to relax, and talking about work does not make me relax at all. I’m off for an entire week. I just hope I don’t have to spend it trapped in the house,” she groaned.

“Damn, I didn’t think I was such bad company.”

Aris outstretched her arms. “No, you’re not. I promise you’re not. To be honest, you’re probably the highlight of my night.”

“So, you lived here for a minute?” he asked, looking around at the minimal Christmas décor throughout her apartment.

“In this apartment or the city?”

“Both, I guess. I know you said you visit your family, so I figured you weren’t from around here.”

“Yeah, I’m not. My hometown is further north, about a five-hour drive from here,” she informed him.

He nodded. “Bet. You live alone? I don’t want no

nigga bustin' up in here on me for spendin' time with his lady."

Aris let out a light chuckle. "If that's your way of trying to figure out if I'm single or not, the answer is yes, I am."

A ghost of a smile crossed his lips while he stroked a hand down his beard. "Damn, you caught me red-handed."

Unable to pick up the conversation where he'd left it, Aris was hit with ten seconds of awkward silence. "So, uh, did you make a Christmas list this year?" She asked, unable to think of anything else to say.

Mohammad shook his head. "Nah, you?"

Aris shrugged. "I kinda did. Not an actual one with tangible things, more like a mental one."

"Oh, word? What's at the top of the list?"

"Dick," Aris thought to herself.

Mohammad's eyebrows rose as another smirk slid across his face. "Oh word?" he asked, followed by a light chuckle.

A groan accompanied the roll of Aris's eyes. She couldn't believe she'd said her private thoughts aloud. "Oh shit, did I say that out loud? Fuck, I'm soooo fuckin' embarrassed. I'm so sorry!"

He shrugged. “Ain’t nothin’ to be sorry for. We both grown.”

She could feel her caramel skin tone turning beet red with embarrassment. “Damn, I can’t believe I did that,” she said, loosely covering her lips with her hand.

“Stop apologizing. You ain’t say nothin’ wrong,” he assured her while taking in all of her with his eyes.

To put it plainly, Aris was simply breathtaking. She was rocking a short platinum blonde fade that reminded him of something he’d seen Eva Marcille wearing at one point in time or another. He was impressed by her lineup and unique design cut into the side of her head, making a bold yet feminine statement. Not many women could pull off a haircut like that, but she wore it well to him. Aris’ French manicure on long, almond-shaped nails told him she was conservative but modern. Mohammad knew just from the oversized flannel pajamas and fuzzy slippers she had on that she hadn’t been expecting company. He admired her slim body type and how her platinum blonde hair color complemented her full dark brown eyebrows. There was an innocence about her that he appreciated. To some, she may have been plain like vanilla ice cream, but lucky for her, vanilla was his favorite. She had a contagious smile and a set of solidly carved thighs he could see himself diving in between if ever given the opportunity.

“So, are DoorDash deliveries the only thing you do?” She asked.

His face soured. “What?”

“I’m sorry if that came out wrong. I’m just asking because I thought about picking it up on the side once but never went through with it,” Aris babbled.

She gave a half shrug, hoping she hadn’t completely stuck her foot in her mouth. Even though they’d just met, she was enjoying his company. “Stop me if I’m just rambling on or you feel like I’m holding you hostage. I don’t want to keep you from getting home.”

“You good, Aris. I’ll stay as long as you want me to. As far as I’m concerned, I’m right where I need to be.”

Aris lifted her chin as a grin creased her face. The fact that he wanted to continue spending time with her so that neither of them would be alone during the snowstorm elevated her energy to an even higher frequency. Instead of responding, she decided to show off her own “homemade” drink for him.

“I want you to taste something,” she told him.

His face slightly lit up. “What do you want me to taste, Aris?”

Warmth spread across her face. “It’s sort of a family tradition. Here, try this,” she said, handing him a glass of her Christmas concoction.

“What is it?”
“Just try it. I think you’ll like it,” she assured

him. Mohammad slowly lifted the glass to his lips. She eyed him closely, trying to decipher whether or not he indeed liked her holiday drink of choice. "Soooo?" She asked, eager for his response.

"This shit is pretty dope. What all you put in it?"

"Uh, let's see—some eggnog at the base, then two shots of Henny, and a few dashes of brown sugar, nutmeg, and cinnamon. It's like Christmas in a cup, right?"

He laughed. "Yeah, Christmas in a cup."

Aris fixated her gaze on his smile. He had the sexiest one she'd ever seen. Being handsome was as effortless as breathing to him.

"Yo, you good?" He asked, derailing her train of thought.

"No. I, uh—I was just thinkin' that I should probably put somethin' on my stomach before I have any more to drink."

"I'm curious, what happens if you keep drinkin'?" He asked.

Mohammad ran his hand down the side of her face, taking in the softness of her skin on his fingertips. He edged closer, gliding his fingertips against her waist before bringing his lips within the same breathing space as hers. Aris was taken by surprise, but it was a pleasant one. Her fingertips galloped through the coarseness of his beard while his hands raced one another down the arch of her back, trying to get to her ass. Mohammad's calloused hands cradled her body as he propped her up on the countertop. Neither of them brave enough to break the transfixing connection they shared through a simple kiss. Falling deeper into the moment, Aris draped her arms around his neck and let her legs engulf his waist. It had been so long since she'd felt a connection with someone that she never wanted the moment to end.

Her chocolate brown eyes popped open when she felt Mohammad take a step back. She happily watched him pull his shirt over his head. Aris smiled to herself while mentally counting each ab muscle. *2, 4, 6…8.* There were eight perfectly sculpted abs stacked on top of each other.

Mohammad stepped back into the spot he'd left and massaged her erect nipples through her flannel top. An effortless moan escaped past her lips. As captivated as she was by everything that was happening at the moment, there was still a part of her that kept telling her she couldn't go out like that.

"Wait, hold up…" she said, gently pulling her body away from his.

"Somethin' wrong?"

Aris quickly shook her head in an attempt to put his suspicions to rest. "No, nothing is wrong. It's just; I don't want you to get the wrong impression that I'm some sort of psychopath that preys on DoorDash delivery drivers."

"I don't think that shit at all," he told her, leaning in to kiss her neck.

Her eyes rolled back inside her head. *"Fuck,"* she thought to herself. He'd found her spot. "Shit, are we really doing this?" she breathed, all her senses on a thousand.

"Feels that way to me," he said, grabbing his dick through his pants.

His dark-eyed gaze tugged at the last bit of willpower she had left. "Do you have a condom?" She quizzed.

"Nah, this was the last thing I expected to be doing when I showed up at your door," he confessed, rubbing the arc of her hip bones with his thumbs.

"That makes two of us…hold on right quick, let me see what I have," she said before hopping off the counter.

Aris didn't want to admit that she knew she'd been harboring an unopened box of condoms next to her weed stash underneath her bathroom sink for months. The stresses of her job didn't leave her much time for a social life. Dating apps weren't her thing, so in the end, she relied heavily on the three different vibrators occupying her nightstand drawer. She walked into the bathroom and closed the door, almost ashamed to look at herself in the mirror. Instead, she dove underneath the sink, cracked open the box, and was sure to check the expiration date before closing the cabinet door.

"You're in luck, I found a con—," she paused, as she made her way back into the kitchen to pick up where they'd left off.

Aris's jaw seemingly hit the floor around the same time his pants did. He was standing in the middle of her kitchen, massaging an erection so big she didn't have a big enough bow to put on it. Without saying another word, Mohammad pulled her in for another kiss while smacking her ass and gripping it tighter. He gently peeled off the remainder of her clothes before placing her back on the counter. She arched her back and parted her thighs while he pulled her body as close to the edge as he could. Aris watched him slide the condom on, secretly patting herself on the back for getting the XL pack all those months ago. He positioned his hands underneath her thighs and slowly inched his way inside her warmth.

Aris's nails dug into the edges of the counter, trying to hold her balance while Mohammad gradually picked up speed, fucking her suspended body in mid-air. His tall frame was hunched over, and his eyes were hazy. He stared at her so intensely; she didn't dare blink.

"Mmm, shit," she moaned.

They were only a few strokes in, and she was already ready to scream his name to the highest of hills. Mohammad slowly dragged his lips from hers while keeping his weight pressed against her chest. He'd officially earned the title of *"Slow Stroke King"* in her book.

Eager to sample everything she had to offer, he asked, "Can I taste that shit? Let me taste that shit."

Before she could muster up the energy to shoot him a nod of approval, Mohammad had already buried his face between her thighs. Aris tossed her head back in pleasure, running the most sensitive parts of her fingers through his braids.

Aris sucked in a sharp breath. "Ooooh."

Mohammad wrote his name forwards and backward against her folds, only stopping to kiss her inner thigh and blow on her throbbing clit. Her juices tasted like honey and lavender. Aris was as sweet as he'd imagined she'd be. Knowing his cunnilingus skills were A-1, he decided to take things to the next level. He rubbed his index and ring fingers down her plump lips before sliding his longest finger inside her. Another one followed soon after. Aris gripped the back of his neck as he repeatedly tickled her G-spot, ready to make her scream his name.

"Goddamn, you wet as fuck," he informed her.

He kissed up her stomach until his lips latched around her left nipple. His hands and tongue worked in tandem, massaging one breast while tongue-fucking the other. Knowing he could no longer fight the urge to climb back inside her, he pulled her off the counter and bent her over the kitchen sink. He hooked his hand around her throat as he drilled in her from behind. Every stroke was delivering the big dick energy he knew she needed. Aris found herself screaming louder than she ever had in her life. He was putting it down like he was making up for lost time, although the two of them had never crossed paths before.

Mohammad leaned in to kiss her neck before placing both hands on her shoulders to drive her body back into his. The way he handled her body was as if he'd known her his entire life. Delicate, yet firm. He lifted her leg on the side of the counter and pushed deeper. His strong hands cupped her ass as he pumped faster. Aris's mouth hung open. He was deliberately stretching her to her breaking point. She was cumming, quicker and faster than she'd ever done before.

"Ohhhh my fuckinnn' Gahh—damn!" She screamed.

*****

IT WAS FOUR hours, five used condoms, and multiple sex positions later before they both decided they'd quenched their thirsts for one another. He'd awakened something in her; *unleashed* something even.

"Who told you to fuck me like that?" Aris asked, desperately trying to catch her breath.

Mohammad shot her a snakelike grin. "Shit, I just wanted to give you what you said you wanted for Christmas."

She grinned while glancing over at her phone that had somehow ended up on the floor amid their shenanigans. It was 1:04 am, and officially Christmas Eve.

"Merry Christmas Eve," she mumbled to him before drifting off to sleep.

Aris woke up the next morning to the sound of her phone vibrating underneath her pillow. She looked down, realizing she was wrapped in nothing but Mohammad's arms and her flannel sheets. She lazily felt around for her phone long enough to press the side button to silence it completely. Two minutes later, the vibrating started up again and then again after that. Frustrated, Aris slipped out of bed with her vibrating phone in hand. She extended her arms wide, giving her body a good stretch before sliding on Mohammad's white tee that was crumpled up on the floor beside her feet. When she finally got around to looking at her phone, she had missed three calls and five texts from Yara. Figuring she was trying to give her an essential update on the lockdown, she quickly called her back.

"Hello?" Aris whispered while tip-toeing out of her bedroom and closing the door behind her.

"Oh my God! It's about time you answered!"

"I'm sorry, I was asleep. It's literally like seven o'clock in the morning, Ya. What's going on at work?" She asked as she plodded along to the kitchen, flicked on the lights, and popped a K-cup into her Keurig.

"You mean to tell me you still ain't turn on the news yet? Check your phone, girl. They finally announced who the three escaped inmates were. I sent you a screenshot of their pictures from the TV. I've never seen any of them before, but apparently, they are dangerous as fuck!"

"None of them have been caught yet?"

"Only one, but he ain't talkin' about where the other two are," she told her. "It doesn't seem like he's connected, but I could be wrong."

"Wow, okay. Hold on and let me look at what you sent," Aris said, pulling her ear away from the phone and pressing the speaker button. "Okay, give me a second. I'm pulling up your texts right now…"

Aris clicked to open the text thread between her and Yara, and her mouth immediately dropped open.

"Did you look yet? Do any of them look familiar to you?" Yara asked.

Aris's eyes bulged with terror. All she could hear was her heartbeat ringing in her ears. "Oh…shit," she mumbled.

"What? What's wrong, Aris? You recognize one of them or somethin'?"

"Ya, I gotta call you back…"

Without waiting for her friend to respond, Aris abruptly ended the call. No matter how hard she tried to tear her eyes away from the screen, she couldn't. What she saw horrified her to the depths of her soul. She was staring right at a mugshot of Mohammad.

"What the fuck…"

*****

SNOW COVERED THE ALLEYWAY as Shaun pushed through the cold wind gusts and sporadic flurries that were still coming down. He gripped his shoulders tight, trying to keep as much body heat inside his clothes as he could. "Only a few more steps," he mumbled.

He rubbed his hands together and then blew warm air into them, trying to ward off any onset hypothermia he may have got by scraping as much snow off his windshield as he could barehanded. He couldn't wait to feel the warmth of the sun against his skin the moment he sank his toes into the warm sandy beaches of Tahiti or somewhere else where the temperature never fell below 75 degrees. He didn't give a fuck. Anything was better than the ice and snowstorm he was facing. The sirens in the background made him walk a little faster. The closer he got to the front of the building, the more his anxiety started to kick in. Guilt and paranoia clawed at his mind.

"Why is he taking so fuckin' long?"

"It's been hours. Why ain't this nigga answerin' his burner?"

"What if this mothafucka is tryna set me up?"

"Am I gon' get my fair cut of this shit?"

"I knew this nigga was gon' fuck this up for me!"

"Fuck...what if he knows it was me?"

*****

ARIS'S HEART RACED with every breath she drew in, knowing that if she went into her room screaming and yelling like a madwoman, she probably wouldn't live long enough to take too many more. Panic coursed through her veins at the mere thought of not living long enough to see another day. She couldn't shake the idea of the police notifying her family that she'd been murdered. She had to play it smart. *"All I have to do is get him out of here. Once he's on the other side of that door, I can call the police,"* she thought to herself. Her eyes traveled over to the drawer that housed her knives, ranging from butter to butcher, and she raced over to it. She wrapped her hands around the base of the only butcher knife she owned and held it tight against her spine. There was no way she was going into the line of fire completely defenseless.

Her shoulder glided against the refrigerator handle as she turned to go down the hallway. She stopped dead in her tracks the moment her bedroom door swung open. Mohammad's eyes fell upon Aris wearing his shirt, and he smiled. He found himself clinging to the thought of seeing her in his clothes for many more days to come. To him, she looked *damn good.*

His smile was warm. "I knew I was missing something."

Aris shot him a blank stare. "W—what?"

"My shirt," he said, arching his back and shooting his arms up toward the ceiling to stretch. His ab muscles flexed, causing Aris to clench the knife behind her back tighter. "You look better in it than I do."

She looked down, forgetting she'd put it on. "Oh, I'm sorry. Let me uh…" she said, taking an uneven step back as the amount of sweat in her palms increased.

Aris could feel the weakness in her knees as she stumbled back a step. His forehead creased. The sun had risen, and he could feel the vibe change between them almost instantly. "Yo, you good?"

"I'm uh—fine. I just, er—I think you should go," she said, fear clawing through her as the seconds passed between them.

"Did you not have a good time last night?" He asked, licking the dried residue of her sweet nectar from his lips.

"I—I did. I just think—the snow stopped, so the roads should be somewhat clear by now. Plus, it's Christmas Eve—and I'm sure you have somewhere to be, just p—*please*, go."

Her arms remained locked tightly behind her backbone as she tried to keep her jaw from trembling. Her brows remained upturned at him as if he'd grown a second head. Something had happened to cause the rupture of bad energy between them, and he needed to know what it was.

When he showed up at her doorstep just the night before, he hadn't expected the events of the night to unfold the way they did. He showed up at her apartment with a job in mind. One that truthfully didn't involve dropping off her dinner. Two things were clear; either she'd found out who he was, or she was genuinely awkward as fuck the morning after fucking a stranger. Before he could fix his lips to respond, he heard her phone vibrate against the kitchen counter. Her eyes bulged wide as she stepped back again.

"Who's that?" he asked.

Aris chewed her trembling bottom lip as the melanin practically drained from her face. *"It's now or never,"* she thought to herself. The deafening silence only grew louder, making the sound of her vibrating phone almost inaudible. In the passing seconds, Aris darted back into the kitchen, swiped up her phone with one hand, and revealed the knife she was holding in the other.

"Stay back! Stay away from me!" She yelled.

His mouth rested in a hard line as he slowly raised his hands in the air. "Aris, who is that on the phone?" He asked calmly.

"Please just leave!"

"Aris, chill and just put the knife down," he said with his palms still raised.

"Or what?"

"Look, I don't want to hurt you, aight?" He said, maintaining balance in his tone.

"Bullshit!" She yelled, waving the knife closer to him. Although she was the one holding the knife, she would've been crazy to think he hadn't seen worse. She had to show him she wasn't going to just roll over and die.

"Just put the knife down, and we can talk all this shit out, I swear. All I need to know is if you told anybody I was here."

"And what if I did, huh? What if the cops are already on their way?"

"If the cops were on the way, you wouldn't be shaking like someone who didn't have someone on the way to rescue her. Just put the knife down, and I promise I'll tell you whatever you want to know."

"You think I'd believe anything you have to say? Your fuckin' mugshot is all over the news!" She shouted, showing him a picture of his mugshot on her phone.

"I can explain," he said, his tone stoic.

"Explain what? That you escaped from fuckin' prison! That your name isn't really Mohammad? Did you target me because I work there, huh? Did you?" She yelled, feeling a range of emotions flooding her body.

“What are you talkin’ about? I didn’t know shit about you before I knocked on your door, and I still don’t. I didn’t come here for you.”

“Then what the fuck did you come here for? Because it wasn’t to bring my food!”

The more she talked, the slower he edged over to her. He knew she didn’t have it in her to cause him bodily harm, but he also knew fear would drive people to do things outside of their nature if they believed their lives were on the line. He’d always been driven by his desires and didn’t have a problem dealing with anyone or anything that got in his way. Unbeknownst to her, Aris was the only thing standing in between him and the red diamond worth twenty million dollars he’d stashed in her apartment seven years prior when *he* rented it. The place wasn’t how he’d left it. The wooden floor was polished to a warm honey gold, new fixtures in the bathroom, and updated appliances. All that remained the same were the two exposed brick walls in the living room and bedroom. The other walls were painted a pristine white. He had no problem giving her the truth she craved, but it would be on his terms. After all, he still had a job to do.

“What time is it?” he asked, changing the course of their conversation.

Her forehead creased. “What?”

By the time she responded, he’d gotten close enough to wrap his hand around hers and gently wrestled the knife from her grasp. When the blade collided with the vinyl kitchen flooring, she hurried back into the corner and quickly pulled up her keypad to dial 9-1-1.

"Give me your phone," he demanded.

"I'm not giving you shit until you tell me the fuckin' truth about why you're here! If you don't tell me in the next three seconds, I'm pressing the call button!" She warned.

The two of them were at a standoff as the tension between them grew hot as a winter campfire. He exhaled a long breath through his flaring nostrils, only seconds away from losing his composure. "I need to make a call."

"I'm not giving you my phone!"

Aris could see her discontent was starting to piss him off, and she flashed herself a mental yellow light to slow down before he slaughtered her like the helpless lamb they both knew she was.

"You swear you didn't tell anyone I was here?" He asked once more, eyeing her closely. He knew a person's eyes would always tell their hand before their lips would.

She slowly shook her head. "No. I—I didn't say anything to anyone, *yet*."

She let that last word fall off her tongue as a threat before telling herself to slow her roll for the *second* time. Fear was one thing, but it was her curiosity that was driving her boldness. She wanted to know the truth behind his deception. There were too many emotions sounding off inside her body at once, making it so she didn't know what to feel. On the one hand, she was fighting flashbacks of his warm kisses laced with Hennessy against her bare skin and cursing herself for thinking he could top her off with some morning wood before venturing out into the cold again. On the other, he was a stone-cold killer. Shit didn't get any more real than that.

"My name is Easton Carruthers. I go by East. I used to rent this same apartment seven years ago before the feds kicked down the door."

Curious, yet still frustrated, she asked, "And what does any of that have to do with me?"

"Not a damn thing."

Her forehead creased with concern. "What?"

"I didn't come here for you. I came for something I left here seven years ago that the feds ain't get when they raided my shit."

Aris loosely folded her arms across her chest. She could feel herself slowly letting her guard down. "And what's that?"

"I can show you better than I can tell you. All I need you to do is trust me."

Unease rolled through her body like a dark wave as she looked down at the knife on the floor. Neither of them had opted to grab it to defend themselves. If he wanted to kill her, she'd already been dead. She'd given him countless opportunities to do so, and he hadn't so much as raised his voice in her presence since she'd confronted him. Trust was something that Aris didn't dish out quickly, yet she found herself always searching for the good in people even if they didn't seem to have any. Unable to say anything thought-provoking, she opted for a simple head nod instead. East turned to go down the hall toward her bathroom. She slowly followed him, stopping in her tracks as she watched him pull all of her things from underneath the sink. A smile tugged at his lips as he removed the false bottom of the cabinet and pulled out a saran-wrapped block of money and a small black crushed velvet pouch.

He held the bag in the palm of his hands and kissed it. "It's still here," he whispered with pure joy laced in his expression.

She broke eye contact with him long enough to try and get a glimpse at what he was holding in his hands. He took the money and the pouch into her bedroom and dropped them on her bed before disappearing into the kitchen. Seconds later, he reappeared with the same knife she'd intended on using on him at one point or another. She watched East split open the money and then open the tie on the pouch before shaking what was inside out onto the bed. Her breath stalled. In the center of hundreds of dollar bills was a shiny red diamond.

"Is this real?" she asked, eyeing the sparkling five-carat jewel in the middle of her unmade bedsheets.

He wore a grin as wide as the ocean. "As real as it fuckin' gets."

Aris admired the way it sparkled in the natural light peeking through her bedroom curtains. "How did you get this?" She spoke timidly, with not as much gusto as she had previously.

"All you need to know is that this is a Moussaieff red diamond, and it's worth at least twenty million dollars."

Aris's jaw practically dropped to her bare knees. "*Twenty million*?" She repeated in disbelief.

"Yeah, if not more."

"And it's been hiding here in this apartment for all this time?"

"Yup. Hold it," he said, placing the triangular cut jewel in her hand.

Aris held the jewel closer to her face, taking in all of its facets. "What the fuck…" she mumbled. "I can't even believe what I'm seeing right now."

"Believe it. You're holding one of the most sought after diamonds in the world in the palm of your hand," he said, observing her closely.

"So that's why you got locked up? You stole a fuckin' diamond?"

East leaned his head against the wall beside her bedroom door. "Believe it or not, that wasn't the original plan."

"Then what was it?" she asked, still unable to fully tear her eyes away from what was in her hand.

"What do you see when you look at me, Aris?" He asked.

She frowned. "What kind of question is that?"

"The kind you need to answer before this conversation goes any further."

Aris studied his face for a few inaudible seconds, taking note of the crease in his brow and the hard stare he was returning to her. "I—I don't know. At first, I thought you were just a fine ass delivery driver who may have been a little rough around the edges, but then I saw your mugshot, plus the fact that you were being held at the same place that helps me keep the lights on here. Now I'm standing here with a fuckin' diamond in my hand...it's all too much, and I—I just don't know."

The muscles in his face relaxed. "You know what I did to keep the lights on here? I was making my way up the ranks as an international arms dealer. This apartment was just one of many residences I utilized at some time or another to conduct my business or, as you can see, house things of importance to me," he told her while zeroing in on the diamond once more.

Her wide-eyed stare made it clear that she was puzzled. "So how'd you get caught?"

"I was young, and I started listenin' to the people around me instead of listenin' to myself and what I knew to be true. I brought too many mothafuckas to the table who wanted to eat off my plate but didn't want to work long or hard enough to sustain their own. It took some time for me to admit that to myself, but it's the truth. I ended up doing business with a black market buyer that one of my soldiers connected me to. When the day came to make the trade, shit just didn't feel right. Paranoia was swallowing me whole, and I made the only move I thought I had left to make."

"Which was?" She probed.

"I put bullets in him and the one who put me on to him and took everything on the table. I intended to become a ghost, but I didn't move quick enough. Less than 18-hours later, the feds raided three of my other residences across the city and then this one. They seized enough shit to lock me up for the rest of my life. It turns out, my paranoia was warranted. I'd been on their watch list for almost a year before they caught up to me. They knew about the deal before I even showed up."

"How?"

"The one that put me on with the buyer was conspiring with the feds behind my back to take me down."

"So where did the diamond come into play?" She asked, falling even deeper into his backstory.

"I found it buried at the bottom of the buyer's bag underneath the quarter of a million dollars he was going to pay me for the weapons. It wasn't a part of our deal, so I knew it wasn't intended for me. I didn't know shit about diamonds, especially not a colored one. I didn't know if it was real or fake, or if it was even worth anything. Once I heard all of my spots were being hit one by one, I knew I wouldn't make it out of the city, so I decided to hide it until I could learn more about it. After I got locked up, I stayed with my head in a book. All I wanted to do was read up on any and everything I could find about red diamonds. That's when I learned that not only was the shit I'd hidden real, but it was worth up to twenty million fuckin' dollars, and that's when I started to put my plan into motion."

"So that's why you and two other guys broke out of prison? To retrieve this?"

"Nah, that's why I broke out. The only people who know about the diamond are standing right here in this room, Aris. What you got in your hand right now, that's my ticket out."

Aris could feel the backlog of questions waiting to explode off her tongue. The more he talked, the more she realized she knew nothing about him. Even what she thought she knew felt like a complete lie. *Was he remorseful for anything he did to get him to where he was? Did he intend to let her live now that he'd told her about the diamond? Who was the man she'd given a piece of herself to?* Not knowing which question to ask next, she parted her lips and let the first one fly out. "Do you regret any of it?"

East shook his head. "I've come too far to regret anything now."

As far as he was concerned, he was on the brink of the only thing he'd been dreaming about for the past seven years, his freedom. The only thing standing in between it all was five-foot-three inches tall with eyes that could turn even the coldest heart warm.

"So no remorse for even one of the lives you took? Guards are dead, East. All for this? Why risk getting thrown back into prison for the rest of your life? Why not serve your time and get the diamond when you legally became a free man?" She queried.

"There's no such thing as being a free man with a life sentence hanging over your head," he informed her.

Her eyes lit up with surprise. "You got life?"

"Yeah. My lawyer tried to get my charges dropped to voluntary manslaughter, but because of who I was and what I did, the odds were stacked against me from the jump. I was a threat. Knowing that, what would you do?" he questioned.

She shook her head. "I don't know what I'd do."

"Most people don't. I guess that's why they tell you to listen to your gut. Had I listened to myself from the beginning, shit would all be different right now."

She shrugged. "I guess."

"I'm not a reckless mothafucka. I don't just go around blowin' heads off for no reason. But you're right; there's one death on my hands that I do regret. The one and *only one*."

"Whose that?" She asked, feeling compelled to dig deeper.

"Remember when I told you that the one that put me on was the one who dropped my name? I was wrong. It wasn't him."

"How do you know you were wrong? Did the feds tell you who the snitch was or something?"

"They didn't have to. After years of putting the puzzle pieces together, I know who it was."

"Who?"

He shook his head. "That's not important; what's important is me getting out of here with what I came here for."

Aris sighed. "But I have more questions."

"You can ask me whatever because you're holding my future in your hand right now; just make it quick," he said, peering out of her bedroom window.

The red diamond she had clasped in her grip had always been his escape plan, but the mindset he had before meeting her had been altered. It was supposed to be a quick transaction. He'd planned to kill whoever was on the other side of that door, get his diamond and be on his way to freedom by Christmas morning. His eyes wandered around her room. Nothing had gone as planned. He may have gotten what he came for, but at what cost? His fingerprints were all over the apartment, and Aris was still breathing. Since his face was plastered all over the news, he knew the feds would soon be on his trail if they weren't already. He had to think of a new plan, and fast. His ears zeroed in on the whirring sirens in the distance. Time was running out. East darted over to her closet in search of a bag to put the money in. His eyes landed on a teal North Face bookbag, and he shoved the cash inside.

His gaze cut into hers. "My diamond."

Aris placed the jewel in his extended hand and continued to watch him pack. She was about to get what she wanted, to get him out of her apartment without being harmed. Yet, she felt like she would be losing a piece of herself she never knew existed as soon as he was on the other side of that door.

"This is your last chance to ask whatever you want to ask," he said, drawing her back into the moment.

Aris drew in a sharp breath. "Okay, so what happened to the real Mohammad since he was supposed to be delivering my food?"

"I left him outside."

Her eyebrows knitted. "Outside where?"

"I needed to get in the building, so when I saw him pull up and run to the door, I approached him, took what he had in his hand, and shoved his ass back out into the snowstorm."

"So you didn't kill him?"

"It was cold as fuck last night, so that young mothafucka might've frozen to death, I don't know. He wasn't my priority, and he still isn't," he said coarsely.

For years, East had accepted that his plan would call for him to get his hands dirty again. There was a bullet with her name on it before they'd ever locked eyes. But he failed to calculate what would happen if he caught feelings for the person on the other side of the door. He hadn't planned to share the rest of his days as a free man with one woman. Yet, there was a part of him that knew he'd regret it for the rest of his life if he parted ways with her.

"I didn't want it to be like this, Aris. When I showed up at your door, I planned to get what I came for and hit the road to Miami before the sun came up. I was supposed to be watching the sunrise while sailing somewhere off in the Gulf of Mexico by Christmas. Then the storm happened…and then *you* happened."

Inspired by his honesty, Aris nodded. "I guess this Christmas isn't going to go the way either of us planned."

He sighed. "Look, we both know shit is too hot for me to move right now. But, if you help me get out of the city when the roads clear…five million is yours," he offered.

He had to get his head back in the game. Nothing could come between him and his independence. She was already too entangled in his web to fight to get out, but he still had to bait her. She knew too much, and he couldn't risk getting caught up a second time. He knew the quickest way to get what he wanted from someone was to make the other person believe they were getting what they wanted. *Everyone* was looking for a come up, whether they admitted it or not.

Aris's head began to spin as her heartbeat quickened in her chest. She could barely believe her ears. That's what she got for wishing for spontaneity. The universe had delivered everything she'd asked for tenfold. "W—what did you say?"

"What is it that you really want, Aris?"

"What do you mean?"

"I mean, you don't dream about shit? You wanna live in this dusty ass apartment forever?"

"No, of course, I don't, I just—"

"You just what?" He cut her off, "because you sound scared to me."

He was like the serpent that tempted Eve in the garden, seducing Aris with his tongue and the pole swinging between his legs. "As long as you stay down and hold up your end of the deal, the money is yours."

"And what if I don't?" She quizzed. Before she said anything, she needed to pose all of the hypothetical questions she could to know all of the outcomes. Her breaths quickened as he stepped closer to her and lifted her chin.

"Let me introduce you to the life you deserve to be livin'."

She returned her gaze to him, instantly slipping

into a trance from the persuasive words dripping off his lips. She knew she should've run, screamed even, but all she could do was stand frozen in his grasp as if her feet had been rooted to the floor. Her lips parted to speak, but nothing came out. Instead, she flinched at the sound of banging on her front door. Her stomach flopped and then tightened with knots. "Who is that? Oh my God, is that the cops?"

Rather than give in to her paranoia, East exited her bedroom and walked over to the front door to look through the peephole. He turned to see Aris inching her way in his direction.

"Who is it?" she whispered.

"That's the reason I needed to make that phone call earlier."

She scrunched her nose. "What the fuck is going on? More secrets? More lies?"

Aris kicked herself for foolishly becoming unguarded again by letting his words and the possibility of becoming a millionaire cloud her better judgment.

He jerked his head toward the door. "Lower your voice, aight? All you gotta do is trust me. I won't let anything happen to you," he assured her.

She watched East go into his jacket, grab a gun and screw the silencer onto the tip before tucking it behind his back. He slowly opened the door. Aris stood in awe at the person standing there. She recognized his face as another one of the mugshots Yara had sent to her phone. *"Shaun Michael Davis,"* she thought to herself. Panic swelled inside her like a balloon. Just when she thought she'd live, death was yet again staring her in the face. The whole situation was the equivalent of taking an espresso shot of anxiety straight to the head. Everything had left her wondering who did she piss off in another life to end up in the predicament she was in less than 24 hours before Christmas?

"Who the fuck is she?" Shaun asked as his eyes narrowed to crinkled slits.

He jammed his hand in his back pocket and pulled out a gun. Aris drew in a harsh breath, fully aware that it could've been her last. Every muscle in her body tightened as her extremities began to tremble all over again. Although he was a small man, his rage was immense, and she had no intentions of testing him.

"She's good. She's with me," East announced, reaching around and placing his hand on the gun.

"Fuck you mean she's with you? That wasn't part of the plan!" He yelled, screwing the silencer onto the tip.

"There's a new plan."

Boiling with fury, he ground his teeth and clenched his jaw before speaking. "Fuck that! We went over this shit a million fuckin' times. You were supposed to kill whoever lived here, get the money, and meet up with me so we could get the fuck out of the city! I didn't risk my freedom for you to get caught up with some bitch!"

"I swear I don't know anything!" Aris yelped, interjecting herself into the conversation.

"Where the fuck is the money, bitch?" Shaun yelled, aiming the gun right in the middle of her forehead.

It had become clear to him that East had switched up. Feeling betrayed, he knew there was no way he was going back to prison to serve another hour, let alone another day. If it came down to it, he'd put a bullet in both of them and skate off with the money East had promised him. Once they escaped, East was supposed to get the money he'd hidden in the apartment and split it with him while Shaun got their fake passports and a vehicle for them to escape in before the sun rose. He'd been parked in an alleyway near the apartment building waiting for East since three o'clock that morning. As far as he was concerned, he'd held up his end of the deal. He wasn't leaving without being paid. Once the money was split, they agreed to go their separate ways. No one expected to be stranded in the city due to the snowstorm.

"I don't know anything about any money! Please! Just listen to what I'm saying! I don't have anything you want!" She yelped. Her voice choked up with tears as her eyes nervously darted over to her work badge that was lying face down beside her purse.

Shaun quickly followed her eyes and walked over to grab it. His eyes glazed over her name, job title, and where she worked. His nostrils flared. "This bitch works at the fuckin' prison? What the fuck happened to no loose ends, huh? Do you remember that? That's what the fuck we agreed to!" He roared, releasing the safety.

"Please, please don't kill me! I swear you can leave right now, and it'll be like I never saw either of you! I won't tell anyone, ever! I swear on my life!" She begged helplessly.

"I know you won't tell anyone because ghosts don't fuckin' talk!"

Aris could hear her heartbeat hammering in her chest as she watched his finger fold around the trigger. In her final moments, one thing had become chillingly clear. East made promises to anyone he intended to use until he got what he wanted. If he could easily switch up the plan with the person he made it with, then the probability that she'd be walking away a millionaire after everything was said and done was slim. Her life was meaningless when it came to his more significant desires. It was either her life or his.

"Did you park the car where I told you to?" East asked, slowly stepping in front of Aris.

Shaun scowled. "I got the car. Don't fuckin' worry about that. What we need to be worried about is why this bitch is still breathin'!"

"What about the passports?" East responded.

"In the glove box, mothafucka! Unlike you, I hold up my end of the deals I make!" Shaun yelled, feeling the heat of anger on his face.

East nodded. "Good to know…"

Aris's heart stopped at the sound of two muffled gunshots ringing through the air. With her eyes slammed shut, she instinctively felt across her chest to see if she'd been hit. When she opened her eyes, she saw Shaun leaking blood all over her carpet, groaning in pain. East had put bullets in both of his knees.

"What the fuck!" He yelled, holding his wounds.

East walked over and kicked the gun away from him. He knew that it was easy for a wise man to play the fool, but a fool could never play a wise man. Instead of quickly ending his life, he decided to take advantage of the opportunity and teach him a lesson before he took his last breath.

"Get on your knees!"

"W—what?"

"You heard me. I said, get on your fuckin' knees before I blow them completely out from underneath you next time."

Silence enveloped the trio as Shaun struggled to hold himself up on his shattered kneecaps. Glaring anger poured from his teary eyes. "Ahh! What the fuck?!" His words were slurred and clipped.

"All I want to know is one thing."

"What?" He cried.

"Why'd you do it? Why'd you snitch?"

"I don't know what the fuck you're talkin' about!"

"Don't play that shit with me! You flipped on me when I helped put food on your table, which means there's nothing you won't do! I want to hear the words come out of your bitch ass mouth!"

When the room went silent again, East pulled the

trigger, letting a bullet graze Shaun's shoulder. He groaned again. "I fuckin' got caught up, aight?!"

"On what?" East asked, pressing the gun against Shaun's temple. "I don't think I should have to remind you that you're on borrowed time."

"L—Look, they tried to pin some child pornography shit on me for talkin' to a 15-year old bitch on a fuckin' dating app. The bitch sent me some pictures and said she was 18. I didn't know she was underage. They—they told me they wouldn't put me on the sex offender's list if I gave you to them. Everything they had on you up until then was circumstantial. They needed something to stick if they were gon' take you down. They wanted bodies."

"So that's why you were feedin' me all that bullshit, pitting me against Kareem and having me paranoid as fuck going into that deal? It was because of you the entire time! You gave me up to save your ass, and yet, you ended up right in the same box as me. How fuckin' ironic is that?"

When Shaun agreed to become an informant, he thought he was doing it to get less time for himself. Unbeknownst to him, he was just a puppet in the FBI's game. Two days after he gave up East's business dealings, the feds were hauling him out of his apartment for conspiracy and sexual crimes that would leave him to face 120 months in prison. When East approached him about his plan, he thought going along with it would prove his loyalty and that he would be able to carry his betrayal to his grave. Shaun blew the air out of his cheeks while gritting his teeth to take the edge off the pain. "I'm sorry, aight? I—I didn't know what else to do."

"The choice was obvious, but you let greed get you caught up," East snarled.

"I—I know. I went along with this plan to show you how loyal I am to you. C'mon, East. It doesn't have to end like this between us. All I want is what I came for, and I swear you'll never see or hear from me again," he begged.

Heat burned his cheeks as he glared down at Shaun without blinking. He'd waited years for that moment. He needed Shaun and the other escaped inmate to play their parts and be the distractions he knew they would be. As far as he was concerned, they were both just pawns in his bigger game of chess. It was never his intent for Shaun to make it out of the city alive. He'd done exactly what East needed him to do, and his job was done.

"If you can walk out of here, the money is yours," East told him.

Shaun's brow creased. "W—what?"

"I'm a man of my word. Here, take it."

East tossed the teal bookbag to Shaun as he struggled to hold himself up. Aris watched as he pathetically leaned against the back of her couch to try and lift his crushed knees off the ground. To no avail, he unzipped the bookbag, caught a glimpse of the money, and smiled. Using his elbows, Shaun army crawled his way over to the door. As soon as his hand began inching its way up to the doorknob, East walked up on him and aimed his weapon at the back of Shaun's head. Two bullets penetrated the back of his skull at close range before he even turned the knob. East leaned down to retrieve the bag. "I'm a man of my word, Shaun. No loose ends," he mumbled.

Aris let out a muffled scream through her covered mouth. There was a dead man in her apartment. No, there was a *dead inmate* in her apartment that just so happened to have escaped from her job. What would the cops say when they found him there? Would they think she was involved? What if she lost her job or worse? She'd gone from feeling like a victim to an accomplice, and she hadn't harmed a soul. Her legs raced to the bathroom, and she heaved into the toilet. When she finally lifted her head, East was standing in the door frame.

"You scared?" He asked.

"Shouldn't I be?" She asked anxiously, wiping her mouth with the back of her hand.

"No, you don't. This situation doesn't have to be all bad."

"You just murdered a man in cold blood in my fucking living room! A man that also happened to escape from the same prison as you did, which just so happens to be the place that I work at! What if the cops think I had something to do with this shit? I could lose my job!

Or worse, I could lose everything and go to prison for something I had absolutely nothing to do with! How is this not a bad situation?" She yelled.

"All you have to do is tell me what you want," he said, taking a glimpse of his reflection in her vanity mirror and wiping specks of Shaun's blood off his cheek and forehead.

"I—it's not that sim—"

"Because if you ask me, I don't think you know," he said, cutting her sentence off at the knees.

She shrugged nervously. "I want the same thing everyone else does. I just want to be happy. I want to live the rest of my life without having to look over my shoulder every few seconds for laws I didn't break! I want to rewind the past 16 hours of my life so that I would've gotten on that plane to see my family and never met you! I want to feel safe, East! I need to feel safe!"

"I can provide safety, but tell me what makes you happy. Because if you were to ask me what I wanted out of life and what would make me happy, I could tell you without a shadow of a doubt."

"And what is that?" She quizzed, folding her arms across her chest.

"Shit, I want to build a new life and buy a string of islands. I want a house on each of them too—my own fuckin' compound like that mothafucka Tyler Perry. Two

Neapolitan mastiffs—Coco and Rocky, as my guard dogs. Also, I want properties scattered in remote locations across the U.S. and its territories. I was a man with connections, on our soil and foreign. I want that power back without having to be in the trenches and risking my freedom again. And I'm willing to give you a piece of all of that."

"Wow…you have it all figured out, huh?" She said sarcastically. "Do you think I'm stupid? You don't care about me! You're going to use me just like you used him!" She yelled, storming past him.

"Shaun's fate was decided long before I met you, so that's irrelevant."

"Shut up! Just shut up! I need to think!" Aris yelled, pacing back and forth down the hallway.

"You can stand there and crucify me all day, but I haven't let harm come your way since you met me, have I?"

"No, but—I…"

"If you can stand here and tell me you don't feel a connection between us, then I'll leave out of your door, and I promise you'll never see me again. But if you do, then all I'm asking for is your help, and I swear I'll change your entire life. You should know by now that I'm a man of my word."

Aris couldn't shake the anxious feeling in the pit of her stomach. "It's just not that simple."

"Why isn't it? All you have to do is say yes," he stressed.

There it was again. His tempting tongue. What would her family say if they ever found out? How would she explain herself to Yara? How would she ever be able to look at herself in the mirror again without feeling the weight of guilt pressing heavily against her chest? After all, she wasn't cut out for the Bonnie and Clyde life, and people lost their lives around him. She didn't want to be the next one on the chopping block whenever he decided she was expendable. Yet, there was a part of her that knew it would be a shame to let a good dick like that wither away behind bars. No matter what she chose, her decision would be consequential. East studied the mayhem across her face as she toyed with her limited choices. To him, it was easy. She could quit her job, hit the road with him, and spend the rest of her days living in the lap of luxury with the best dick of her life. Freedom was right around the corner for both of them.

"I can't think this hard under pressure," she said, pounding her palm against her forehead.

"The fact that you have to think about it already lets me know what your answer is going to be."

"Yes, I'm torn! Do I want to be stupidly fuckin' rich and never have to worry about money ever again? Yes! Do I think this is a terrible fuckin' decision that could land me in prison for the rest of my life? Also yes! I can't make a big decision like this so easily! I'm not perfect, okay?!"

“I’m not asking you to be perfect, Aris. I’m asking you to be smart,” he told her.

Aris sighed. She was left with two choices; uphold her civic duty and turn in the man who’d turned her entire world upside down and risk the cops thinking she was involved in it from the beginning, or take him up on his offer and spend the rest of her days as a millionaire waiting for the other shoe to drop. East walked over to Shaun’s body and patted down his pockets until he found the car keys.

“If the roads were clear enough for him to get here, then they should be clear enough for us to go. What’s it going to be, Aris? Are you coming with me or not?”

Aris’s breath hitched. He’d put her on the spot yet again, and she didn’t know what to say. Caught between a rock and a hard place, she needed a blunt in hand to calm her nerves and help her figure out her next move. On the one hand, risk-taking was the quickest way to the grave or prison. On the other, her inability to be spontaneous was one thing she hated the most about herself. Yeah, she smoked weed, but going on the run with the likes of a very handsome, very dangerous stranger was out of her nature. She’d always adhered to routine, being sure never to color too wildly outside the lines. She’d been wired to think that way since she was a child. She and her brother Desmond were brought up to see the danger in everything.

She looked at the dead body and the bloodstains

soaking into her carpet. In *her* apartment. Large streaks of blood were caked and hardening by the minute. How would she even begin to explain that? Aris knew law and order took precedence over the truth in America. There was no way she could risk telling the police the truth about what happened and not being believed. Keeping the secret was best for them both, so she decided that she wouldn't tell a soul.

"What are we going to do about him?" She asked, pointing at Shaun's lifeless body.

East's nostrils flared, knowing his body would start to smell if they didn't move him. He looked around her apartment until his eyes landed on her suitcase that was still packed and standing by the door.

"Empty your suitcase," he told her, "I have an idea."

Aris frowned. There were parts of her that wondered how she'd mentally process everything she'd witnessed in so little time. Rewriting the truth in her mind would be the only way she'd be able to cope with the mental numbness.

"Wh—"

When she didn't move immediately, East walked over to the suitcase, unzipped it, and shook her belongings out onto the floor. Aris stood back and watched him drag Shaun's limp body over to the suitcase. As large as her suitcase was with nothing inside it, she wasn't sure his body would fit inside, let alone close.

"Are you sure this will work?" She asked, watching East stuff Shaun's folded body into the suitcase.

He shot his eyes toward her. "If there's no body, there's no homicide. They'll just continue looking for him as if he's still on the run. *If* they ever find his ass, we'll be long gone."

"Okay, so what do we do with him if you can get all of him inside there?"

"Isn't there a trash can in the alleyway?" He asked.

Aris nodded. "Y—yeah. If you go to the end of the hall by the elevators, there's a window overlooking the alley. There's an open trash bin directly underneath the window that people drop their bags in all the time instead of having to go downstairs to take their trash out physically."

"Good, I want you to wheel him down there with a bag of trash, open the window and drop that mothafuckin' suitcase right into the trash while I clean this shit up."

"Even if I could wheel him down there, I can't lift him by myself! He's a whole person!"

East sighed. "Aight, bag up your trash and give it to me. I'll do it, and you start cleaning up."

*****

WHEN EAST RETURNED, Aris was on her hands and knees trying to scrub the crimson bloodstains out of her carpet. This left him to start mopping up the dried blood and wiping his and Shaun's fingerprints off any and everything he could think of. It needed to be as if neither of them had ever stepped foot in that apartment. They both turned their attention to the TV when the news reporter came back onto the air.

"New York police are still looking for thirty-two-year-old Easton Carruthers. Authorities say he and Shaun Davis are wanted on multiple charges for their roles in the shooting death of two correctional officers and escaping federal custody. Suspects are considered to be armed and dangerous. If you have any information, please call Crime Stoppers."

"Fuck," he mumbled, "We can't drive. I gotta catch a flight."

Aris stood to her feet, fingering the thin gold chain around her neck as she stared at him. "If you want even the slightest chance of making it out of here, you're not going to make it like that. Your face is everywhere," she said, pointing to the TV.

He ran his hand over his hair. "Fuck," he mumbled again. He'd initially planned to make his escape in the dead of night, yet the sun was high in the sky, and he was still a very wanted man. "You got a hat or somethin' I can put on?"

"No, but I got something better, but before I agree to help you, I need to know what the plan is."

"All you need to know is that I have to be in Miami in the morning."

"On Christmas Day?!" She piped up.

"Yeah."

"And all I have to do is make sure you get to Miami, and that's it? The money is mine?"

"That's the deal."

She nodded. "Okay…"

"Okay? Is that a yes or—"

Knowing she didn't have the time to explore multiple options, Aris straightened her rigid posture while clearing her throat. "It's a yes. I want in—I, I'll help you. Follow me," she said, scurrying down the hallway and into the bathroom.

East followed her, stopping when he saw her with a pair of clippers in her hand. "I was thinking more of a haircut," she told him.

He frowned. "You know what you doin' with them clippers?"

"Relax, I do have a short haircut. Who you think lines me up? I do it myself."

Impressed, he nodded and sat on her closed toilet lid. Aris unbraided his hair, combing her finger through it. "Where's your phone? We need to go ahead and book the first plane tickets to Miami we can get. Get the first shit you can find. Whatever the cost is, I got you."

Aris grabbed her phone and opened her travel app. "Looks like the earliest flight to Miami is leaving in three hours," she told him.

"Book that shit. Two first-class tickets."

Aris was mentally running on autopilot as she moved forward with booking the tickets. She hadn't expected to find camaraderie in a stranger, let alone drop her panties for him the very first night. Yet, there was a growing part of her that had become accustomed to the rollercoaster ride she'd been on since he showed up at her doorstep.

"So we get to Miami, and then what?" She asked over the whirring of the clippers.

"If everything goes according to plan from here on out, it'll be a beautiful fuckin' payday for the both of us."

"You've got every detail planned out, huh?"

"My life is a game of chess, Aris."

"How so?"

"The way my mind works, I weave a billion webs

and play out all of the different possibilities before making my move. You're the only thing I didn't see coming," he admitted.

"Is that a bad thing?"

"Not anymore," he said.

The truth was he needed her. He would be way more inconspicuous traveling with a female by his side instead of on his own. The authorities would be looking for two males, but not a man and a woman.

*****

"I'M DONE," SHE SAID, inching around to look at him from all angles. She'd successfully concealed his facial tattoos with some makeup and given him a cut so fly he looked like an entirely new man. There was an air of readiness about him. In her eyes, he was breathtaking. He looked at her, and she instantly felt a flutter in her belly. Though her brain knew better, her heart and the throbbing between her thighs didn't seem to get the memo whenever they locked eyes.

His lips parted slightly as he snaked his tongue out to lick them. "How a nigga look?"

"Perfect. Good as hell. Like a mothafuckin' caramel Adonis." She thought without parting her lips.

"You look, uh...you look good," she told him

with a smile.

"Bet. Thank you," he said, tapping her phone to see the time. "We need to go."

"Okay, just let me pack a new bag first."

East nodded. "Pack light," he warned her, "you won't need a lot of clothes where we're going."

Aris nodded. "Okay."

"What kind of car do you drive?"

"A black Honda Accord," she told him.

"Give me your keys. Where'd you park it?"

"Maybe a half a block away from here, why?"

"I need to swing by the car Shaun brought and grab what I need, and we'll take yours to the airport. Meet me at your car in five minutes."

"I'm not ready yet. I—I need to smoke before we go. I'm a nervous fuckin' wreck, okay? Trust me; if I'm leaving this apartment, you'll want me to be calm. My keys are by the door."

With his lips pressed firmly together, he nodded. "Do your thing, just hurry up," he said, jingling Shaun's car keys in his pocket.

Aris nodded. "Okay, I will."

*****

SPARSE SNOW FLURRIES STARTED to fall as East headed to the alleyway. He pressed the key fob and saw the lights on the car Shaun had gotten for them light up. He smiled to himself, knowing Shaun had followed his directions to the T. He'd come into the apartment barking and being all hostile just to be a yes man in the end.

"Bitch ass nigga was all bark and no bite," East mumbled to himself.

He hurried to the passenger side and popped open the glove box to grab his passports, one for the U.S. and the other for the dual citizenship in the United Kingdom under his new alias. Easton Carruthers would be no more; he was a ghost in the wind from that moment forward. He slammed the car door, letting loose snow hit the ground. There was still a bit of snow on the salted roads, but it seemed manageable enough to get to their destination.

A gust of icy air seeped through Aris's jacket, making her shiver and encouraging her to pick up the pace to her car. The motor sputtered and whined as she touched the snow-covered door handle to the driver's side door, feeling the frost of winter against her hand. The car had gotten warm enough to start melting the barrier of ice on her windshield so that she could see East sitting in the passenger seat.

She climbed inside and rubbed her gloved hands

together for warmth before gripping the steering wheel. Aris found herself shifting in her seat every few minutes, unable to remain comfortable for too long. All she could do was pray to God their flight didn't have any delays. As soon as she got to her first red light, she looked in the center console and noticed not one but two passport books.

"What are your plans to see how much the diamond is worth, and how are you going to sell it? I mean, where do you even go to sell something like that? The black market or the dark web?" She asked.

East only cast a short glance at her before focusing his attention back on the road. "Don't worry about it. I got it handled already," he assured her.

She didn't need to know more than she needed to. Discussing too much information wasn't good for either of them.

"That's it? That's all you're going to tell me?"

"That's all you need to know. Besides, the less you know in all of this, the better."

"Fine," she said, taking her eyes off the road only long enough to see heaps of snow piled on the sides of the road and in vacant lots.

He sighed. "I did my research, aight? And I located an appraiser in Miami that specializes in colored diamonds."

With her phone in hand, he went to her internet browser app and typed in the name *"Vlado Marković."*

"So he's pretty legit then?"

"Yeah, he's been doing this shit for fifteen years. He's verified."

East had used a smuggled burner phone in prison to find the appraiser. He'd already done the legwork in corresponding with him and set up the meeting in Miami. He planned to meet with him to find out the diamond's actual value and sell it to the highest bidder by the new year. *"Sell the diamond, get the money, and get the fuck out of the country. That's the plan. Sell the diamond, get the money, and get the fuck out of the country,"* he repeated to himself.

*****

DESPITE THE SNOW FLURRIES and building holiday traffic, Aris and East arrived at the airport and pulled into the first available parking spot she could find before killing the engine. "We're really doing this, huh?" She asked, heart pounding like crazy in her chest.

East reached out and put his hand on her thigh, feeling it tremble under his grasp. "I need you to relax."

"I can't," she said, gripping her seasick stomach. "I think I'm going to be sick."

"You can, and you will. Now, let's go," he said, eyeing the time on her phone, "our flight boards in an hour."

With only two carry-ons in tow, the two of them made their way to the terminal. Aris walked militantly with her hands squeezed into tight fists to keep them from shaking. Just when they got to the terminal's automated glass door entrance, they saw a beggar sitting outside with a sign and a hat with a few crumpled up dollars inside. Instead of rushing by like everyone else, East walked up and dropped two one-hundred-dollar bills in his cap.

"God bless you, sir," the man's voice echoed behind them.

Aris shot a half-smile in East's direction. "That was sweet of you."

"I can have a heart when I want to."

She bobbed her head. "I see."

As enticing and still mysterious as he was, she realized one thing was true when it came to him. She couldn't judge a book by its cover. On their way to airport security, Aris realized that being high had only made her more paranoid. All she could do was think about all the worst-case scenarios and let them play out in her mind one by one as the line inched along. The lines were long with people trying to reschedule flights due to the snowstorm, everyone still hoping to make it somewhere by Christmas. Time felt like it was dragging as her gaze ping-ponged, avoiding direct eye contact with anyone. Her only hope was that travelers would be too preoccupied with their own rescheduled holiday travel plans to make him out in a crowd.

"Yo, you good?"

She tore her eyes away from her shoes long enough to look up at him. "No."

"Say what's on your mind."

"A million things are running through my mind right now. I wouldn't know where to start," she admitted.

"Chill. You didn't do anything wrong, remember? No one is looking for you; just be calm," he whispered, his breath tickling her ear.

The closer they got to the TSA agent, the more her hands fidgeted. Unable to settle them, she rubbed her clammy hands into the middle of her forehead and tried taking deep breaths. From the crackling of a security officer's radio to luggage wheels skating across the heavily trafficked floor and growling airport police dogs standing by, she was too tuned in to her surroundings to relax. *"Just make it on the plane. All you have to do is make it on the plane,"* she mentally coached herself.

"Next," the TSA agent said, waving them down to her lane.

Aris and East headed in her direction and handed her their boarding passes and identification. The agent looked her up and down. "Miss Donahue?"

"Yes, that's me," she said, unsure if she was blinking as often as she should've been.

"Enjoy your flight, and happy holidays."

Aris nodded. "Yes, th—thank you. Happy holidays to you too."

They both got their bags and headed in the direction of the gate. Aris took a brief sigh of relief. Although they'd made it through security, she was still battling the wave of nausea inside her stomach while walking through the terminal on eggshells. The second she looked up at the TV screen inside one of the airport restaurants, she saw his mugshot plastered clear as day. "Shit, shit, shit," she mumbled, gripping his hand.

His eyes quickly scanned the area. There were two officers with dogs approaching them on the opposite side of the moving sidewalk they were gliding on. "Kiss me," he said, turning to face her.

"What?"

He brushed his hand across her cheek. "Trust me."

East leaned in and pressed his lips against hers for ten, long seconds. By the time she'd opened her eyes, they'd passed by the dogs and security and remained unscathed.

With his head low, East looked into her eyes. “The hard part is over, aight? Go splash some cold water on your face and grab a coffee or somethin’. We still got a few minutes before they start the boarding process. I’ma go to one of these electronic stores and get a phone. I’ll meet you at the gate.”

She nodded. “It’s gate 42,” she told him.

“Okay.”

Feeling dizzy, Aris knew she needed to get her bearings. The police had gotten too close for her liking. When she made it into the women’s restroom, she immediately placed her hands under the automatic sink, closed her eyes, and splashed some cold water on her face. Her eyes opened to the sound of her vibrating phone in her back pocket. She pulled it out and sat it on the edge of the sink. Yara was calling. “Fuck,” she mumbled, unsure if she should answer or not.

Aris drew in one last deep breath before clearing her throat and answering. “H—hello?”

“Aris, why didn’t you call me back? Is everything good?” Yara yelled into the receiver.

She nodded, pulling the phone away from her ear. “Y—yeah, everything is fine. I’m getting on a flight after all.”

“What? Really?”

“Yeah, um, the roads cleared up, so I’m back at the airport.”

“Damn, it must be a Christmas miracle because the prison isn’t on lockdown anymore. They’re letting us go home *finally*,” she stressed. “I’m in the car heading home now.”

“Oh, really? Did they uh catch—you know, the guys who escaped?” Aris asked, fishing for any information that may have been vital to her survival.

“Nope, no updates past what I gave you earlier. If their asses were smart, they’d be far away from the area by now.”

“What are the odds that people who escape from prison end up getting captured again anyway?”

“Girl, I don’t know. What kind of weird-ass question is that anyway?”

Aris sighed. “Sorry, I’m tired, and I don’t even know what the hell I’m saying at this point. I need some coffee in my system pronto.”

Yara chuckled before sounding off on her car horn. “Get the fuck up the road, asshole! Sorry girl, yeah, you do.”

Aris cracked a slight smile. “Listen, my flight is about to start boarding any second now, so uh, I gotta go.”

"Okay, girl, I'm happy you're getting out of here. As hard as you work, you deserve to have a relaxing Christmas."

Aris smiled. "Thanks. You have a good Christmas too," she said before hanging up and exiting the bathroom.

Every flash of movement seemed to catch her eye as she followed the smell of freshly brewed coffee to the nearest coffee shop. Cream swirled in her coffee as she made her way over to East, who was already in line to board the plane. Standing behind him, she pulled out her phone and snapped her bag shut. Her heart began thumping loudly inside her chest again as she tried to anchor her attention to her mobile boarding pass. She knew she wasn't ready for a life filled with paranoia, guns, and shady business deals, but she was too deep in to turn back. *"As soon as we're in the air, everything will be okay. You got this, Aris. Get to the plane, and you got this,"* she thought.

Aris held up her phone and scanned her boarding pass. "Have a safe flight," the gate agent told her."

"Thank you—you too—" she said, stopping herself. She'd nervously told the woman to have a safe flight knowing damn well she wasn't going with them. *"Keep it together, Aris. You're almost there."*

*****

ONCE THEY BOARDED the plane and found their seats, Aris leaned against the seat and crossed her ankles in front of her.

"Where's one place you've always wanted to travel to?" She asked, ignoring the airline's instructional video playing on the headrest in front of them.

East shrugged. "I always wanted to travel the world. I never wanted the grass to grow underneath my feet, you know? Ever since I was a kid, I knew I wasn't destined to stay in one place forever."

"Wow, you've known that since childhood? I feel like I never even really wanted to travel faraway places until I at least turned twenty-five."

He smirked. "Sounds like you've got a lot of catching up to do."

"Yeah, I know. I can only ever remember us going to Disney World once when I was maybe twelve or thirteen. Anything other than that was just random road trips to a nearby amusement park or beach. Did you vacation a lot when you were younger?"

"Nah, I moved around a lot."

"Military?"

"Homeless," he corrected her.

Sinking into her seat a bit, Aris twisted her lips to the side. "I'm sorry, I—"

"Nah, you good. I don't belong anywhere, and I like that shit. Staying in one place too long only brings trouble."

As bold as his statement was, she could hear the hurt in his voice. "I imagine experiencing something like that really made you grow up fast," she said, unknowingly putting her work hat on.

East dragged his eyes over to hers. "You really tryin' to take it there?"

She shrugged. "If I'm being too invasive, you can tell me to back off. I know I ask a lot of questions, and sometimes I pry too much. I'm sorry, it's just the way I'm wired."

"What do you mean?"

"I—I don't really know how to explain it. I'm what you call a bit of an empath, I guess. I can listen to someone's story, and I'm able to put myself in their shoes and understand their feelings while completely leaving my perspective at the door. It's a gift and a curse, trust me," Aris admitted.

Growing up, she'd been molded to talk about her feelings and listen with an open mind and heart about what others had to say about how they were feeling. It was only fitting that she double majored in psychology and sociology when she went off to college.

"How so?"

"Well, for starters, I care too much. I get overwhelmed easily because I get to know people, and I begin to take on their feelings. Too much outside stimuli gets my brain going haywire, and I start to feel overloaded, so—"

East reached over and gripped her thigh. Like a magnet, she drew closer to him. "You know what I used to do when I was scared or grappling with a decision?"

"What?"

"I was raised by my grandmother between the ages of like five and sixteen. And anytime I would get into trouble or fuck up in school, she'd sit my ass down and tell me that my life was my little red wagon and *'either you gon' push it or pull it,'*" he said.

Aris chuckled. "Wait, what?"

"She meant that I was in control of my life, and either I was going to take life by the horns or let it drag me. So anytime I had to make a decision, no matter how hard, if the good outweighed the bad, then I was gon' take life by the horns and do the shit."

She smiled. "Wow, that's a pretty dope message. Thank you for sharing that with me."

He nodded before closing his eyes. "Yeah."

"But wait—earlier you said you were homeless.

Was that before you started living with your grandmother?"

"My mom drug me around from place to place every few weeks or so. Until one day, she scraped up enough coins to get a couple of bus tickets and took me to my grandmother's house. She took me there when I was five and never came back, aight?"

"What ever happened to your mom, if you don't mind me asking?"

East let out a short breath. "If I answer this, this is the last question from you, aight?"

"Deal." Aris nodded.

"Look, a year or so later, I found out she'd left town with a kingpin, married his ass, and never looked back. By then, I was pretty much over the shit. My grandma ended up being both my mom and my dad. She did her best with me, but the older I got, the wilder I became. Until one day, I guess she'd had enough, and she was like fuck it, only God can save you. She kicked me out, and I've been on my own ever since. End of story."

"Wow." Aris nodded, mentally noting how fiercely independent he was. While he'd grown up fending for himself, practically begging to be loved, she grew up under the wings of overprotective, overbearing parents who had almost made her scared of everything.

"Growing up, my parents made all of my

decisions. They taught my brother and I to fear everything so that we'd never get into trouble. '*Don't do this, or you'll go to jail. Or don't hang with them because they'll lead you down a path of destitution.'* They were constantly hovering over me for years, drilling into me the idea of '*Go to school, get a good job, get the husband and settle down.'* Do things the *'right way,'* or whatever that means. My brother has two kids, got married straight out of college, and now he's miserable. You can see it in his eyes, but he wouldn't dare go against how we were raised.

I mean—my parents literally almost had a heart attack when I moved so far away, but I needed to put a comfortable distance between us, though, you know? Over the years, it's gotten better to the point where I can say I actually miss them. I think that's why the holidays are so important to me because it's the only time I carve out of my life to see them."

"Yo, you good now that you got that off your chest? Because I'm tryna take a nap," he said, lowering the shade on the window.

She twisted her lips and frowned. "All I'm sayin' is I'm here if you wanna talk."

"Aris, I'm good, aight? I'm alone because I choose to be alone. I don't need a therapist to vent to or a shoulder to cry on. I'ma take any tears I got inside me straight to the bank. That's all I'm focused on right now, not whatever you're on."

“That may be true, but that doesn’t mean it’s right,” she reminded him.

“Trust me; it’s the best thing for me. Mothafuckas will always choose themselves when times get hard. I’ve seen it happen too many times, shit, I’ve done it.”

Aris found it in her best interest to just nod without offering a verbal response. He’d made it clear she’d worn out her welcome in his brain, and she needed to stop picking. She hadn’t expected their conversation to be filled with so much candor and transparency in the first place. Although he hadn’t shared every single detail of his past, she was glad to know what she did. He’d been open enough to show her one of his many invisible wounds, and she was grateful for that.

East had been abandoned at a young age, which made him think if he allowed himself to get too attached to one person, place, or thing, that would only result in him getting hurt. He’d put his trust in the wrong people all his life and had only been let down when he looked out for them. Aris knew that being abandoned by the first person, he’d ever learned to trust made him look at people differently. There was something inside her that made her want to see everything through with him. The more time she spent with him, the more willing she became to ride it out with him until the wheels fell off or they were both being carried away in the backseat of a cop car. Either way, she became more comfortable with the thought of becoming his ride or die.

Aris turned her attention to the flight attendant coming down the narrow aisle with a drink cart. "Do you want anything?" She whispered before turning to look at him.

One glance at him, and she found herself grinning from ear to ear. He'd fallen asleep the moment the plane had accelerated at takeoff. Her eyes soaked him in. From the way his long eyelashes sat perched against his closed lids to the designer stubble on his face, she found everything about him undeniably attractive.

"Um, excuse me. Can I get a blanket?" Aris asked the attendant. There was always something so comforting to her about the weight of an airplane blanket, and she needed all the comfort she could get.

"Yes, sure. I'll be right back with that."

After receiving her blanket, Aris adjusted her head against the headrest and closed her eyes. As anxious as she was, she needed the rest. *"Just hold on a little while longer. We're almost in the clear,"* she thought to herself before letting the steady sound of the engine take her off to dreamland.

*****

AS SOON AS their flight landed, they took an Uber to a self-storage facility. East pressed in a code, and Aris followed him to a nearby outdoor unit. She cautiously watched him twist a code into a lock before hearing it click.

"Hold this," he said, handing her his bag.

She grabbed it while he lifted the storage door. To her surprise, there was a blacked-out Mercedes sitting inside. East smiled before walking up to it and opening the car door. "Get in."

Once inside, he started the engine with a push of a button. There was a full tank of gas and a gun placed under the driver's seat in a holster, bullets and all.

Aris's eyes widened. "What do you need that for?"

"It's my security blanket. Now sit back and relax. We've got about a forty-five-minute drive ahead of us before we can post up for the rest of the night."

*****

GENTLE WAVES CRASHED against the rocks at the marina as East put the car in park the next morning. After tucking his gun in his pants and securing the diamond in his pocket, he turned his attention to Aris. "Wake up."

"W-what?"

"I said wake up, Aris. We're here."

Aris cracked her eyes open slowly and looked

around. The sun was reflecting off the deep blue waters as the breeze blew against the rocking waves. "Where's here? Where are we going?"

"There," he said, pointing to one of the various-sized yachts lined up at the water's edge.

"What? Whose yacht is that?"

"I need you to stay here, aight?" he said, peeling off his coat. It was 45 degrees warmer there than where they'd flown from.

"Stay here and do what? How long are you going to be gone?"

"However long it takes, okay? Just stay here and keep watch. Hand me your phone."

Aris handed him her phone and watched him type his new number on her keypad and press the call button. "If you see anything suspicious, I want you to text the fire emoji to this number, aight? Can you do that?"

"Y—yeah, I can."

"Good. I'll be back."

East stepped out of the car and walked down the concrete sidewalk that ran alongside the waterway. The closer he got to the 60-foot pearly white yacht, the more he could taste his freedom. He made his way onto the narrow, wooden dock stretching out onto the water and then across the ladder-like walkway onto the boat's entrance. East drew in a deep breath, inhaling the warm ocean air before looking around at the glazed cherrywood interior and cream leather sofas in his sightline.

"Hello," A male voice chimed in from behind him.

East turned to see a man standing a few feet away from him. Recalling his headshot on his website, he knew he was the appraiser he'd come there to meet. "Hello."

"Merry Christmas."

"Same to you." East nodded.

"Do you have the diamond?" he asked, his heavy Serbian accent tearing through his voice.

"I do."

"Then let's get down to business, shall we? Follow me."

East followed the man into a back-office filled with various microscopes and other special testing equipment. He stood back and watched him slide on a pair of gloves before putting on his glasses and turning on a bright LED light. "Do you inspect all diamonds on boats?" he asked.

"I do most of my work at my shop, but it's the holidays, and I enjoy a change of scenery every once in a while just like the next man."

"This is your boat?"

"Yes, it is."

Being that he'd done his research on appraisers and gemologists in the area, East didn't think their salaries alone could afford such a luxurious boat. He knew he had to have a hand in other dealings. Legal or illegal, he wasn't sure.

"I know in our previous discussions you said you've been doing this for several years," he said, handing him the bag with the diamond in it.

"That is true. I've been working with precious stones and gems all my life. My father was a jeweler in a small shop in Flushing, Queens. My siblings and I grew up apprenticing under him."

"What brought you all the way out here?"

"The warm weather." He smiled. "As much as I loved my father, I knew I wanted to be bigger than him, so I studied gemology for years in hopes of becoming my own boss and opening my own business. Fifteen years later, here we are."

East nodded. Their conversation made him feel like his diamond was in capable hands. All he needed to know was how filthy rich he was going to become. He watched as the diamond slid out of the bag, naturally sparkling under the light.

"Ah, the Moussaieff red diamond. You'd be surprised how many people still try to pass off fake diamonds as authentic, but this…this is the real deal," he said, eyeing the diamond closely underneath his microscope.

During his inspection, Vlado took note of the engraved serial number on the diamond, *80382031*. He knew that number like the back of his hand. He'd been searching for it for years. "I'm always fascinated to know how my clients acquire their gems. How did you procure such a rare and precious stone such as this one?" he asked.

"Family heirloom," East replied, not missing a beat.

"It is truly exquisite and worth quite a pretty penny."

"How much are we talking?"

"Millions, easily."

"Give me a hard number."

"I could see it going for no less than 28 million U.S. dollars."

East was instantly floored. He just knew his pupils had dilated to dollar signs or money bags. Keeping his composure in check, he asked, "Do you know anyone in the area who would be interested in buying it? I'm looking to get it off my hands pretty soon."

"Actually, I do. Not only am I a gemologist, but I'm also a collector of scarce gems just like this one."

East's eyebrows knitted. "*You* want to buy this?"

"Oh, absolutely. To show you how serious I am, I can get you ten million in cash and have the rest wired to you in the next couple of hours. Just let me move some things around first."

"How soon can you get the ten million to me?"

"Within the hour. If we have a deal, then you can make yourself comfortable on my yacht, and I'll be back with the money."

East eyed him closely before reaching out to shake Vlado's extended hand. "You've got yourself a deal."

"Excellent. It looks like we both will be having a merry Christmas. I'll be back as soon as I can."

Vlado led the two of them out onto the main deck before exiting the boat. Toying with the diamond in his hand, East replayed their conversation repeatedly in his mind while listening to the waves crash against the side of the boat. The more time passed, the more an uneasy feeling settled in the pit of his stomach. He pulled out his phone to call Aris.

"You good out there?"

“Everything is good,” she replied. “I saw someone walk off the boat a while ago. Why did he leave, and why are you still on there?”

“Our business isn’t done yet.”

“Where is he going?”
“To get my money.”

“What? *He’s* buying the diamond from you? Just like that?”

The way the words fell off her tongue only solidified the eerie feeling in the pit of his stomach. Instinctively, he reached for his gun while his mind clicked away at what his next move would be. “We need to leave,” he said, making his way to the exit.

“Wait, he’s—someone is coming back onto the—h—hello?” Aris asked.

East quickly hung up the phone when he saw Vlado standing on the edge of the dock with a briefcase in hand.

“Leaving so soon? I thought we had a deal.”

“We do,” East said, eyeing him closely.

“Good.”

Vlado opened the briefcase so that East could see the money. Even after seeing the one thing he’d been dreaming about for years, he still couldn’t relax.

Something just wasn't right.

"As promised, here is the ten million in cash. All you need to do is provide me with your bank information, and the rest of the money will be wired to you."

East nodded, providing him the information to his offshore account. The two fell silent for a few seconds while Vlado pulled up his phone and typed in the information. Just before he pressed send, he looked up at East.

"Before we do this, there is something I wanted to ask you."

"What is that?"

"You said the diamond was a family heirloom, right?"

"Yeah."

"I noticed the serial number on the diamond during my inspection, and it's a familiar number."

East clenched his jaw. "How so?"

"My family used to be in possession of the same diamond you're trying to sell back to me. Imagine me spending millions of dollars for something that is already mine."

He glared at him without blinking. "I don't know

what the fuck you're talking about."

"Allow me to bring you up to speed. The diamond that has been in your possession was my brother's."

East's gaze remained locked as he gritted his teeth for control. "You got your diamond, and all you have to do is finish the transfer, and I'll have my money. After that, our business is done."

His face soured. "I don't think it is, you see—I'll be leaving here with both my money and the diamond you stole from my brother the night you killed him in cold blood seven years ago. I've been waiting years for this moment—and I've killed others for less in search of this. And to my surprise, one day, I get an email from you inquiring about a rare gem that had come into your possession. I wasn't sure it was the diamond I'd been searching for all of these years until I saw that serial number. And now that I have it back, killing you will just be the icing on the cake to avenge the senseless murder of Andrej!" He yelled, pulling out his gun.

East quickly put his hands up, knowing all it would take was one wrong move, and his body would be ambushed with bullets. With his heart thudding in his chest, he drew his attention to another man emerging from the back of the boat with a gun in his hand. *"Fuck,"* he thought to himself.

*****

ARIS FELT THE vibrating of her phone in her hand and looked at the screen to see her mother calling instead of East. *"Fuck,"* she whispered before looking around. As much as she knew not to answer, she also knew her mother would call time and time again if she didn't.

"H—hello?" Aris answered, clearing her throat.

"Merry Christmas, baby. How are you?"

"Merry Christmas, Mama. I'm good, I—"

"Wait, do I hear water in the background?" Her mother asked, cutting her off.

Aris's eyes darted out of the window to see the waves rolling against the tide. "No, Mama. that's just the TV."

"Oh, okay. How are you doing? Is it still snowing there?"

Aris eyed the long palm trees swaying in the air as a smile crept across her face. "Yeah, a little. What's it doing over there?"

"Nothing anymore, thank God. I've got to go out and get a few more sweet potatoes for my pies. Your father didn't pick up enough when he went to the store before the storm."

"Oh, okay. I could definitely go for a slice or three of your homemade sweet potato pie right about now."

"If I could mail it to you, I would," her mother assured her.

She smiled a lopsided grin and focused her eyes back onto the yacht that East had disappeared into. Seconds later, gunshots rang out, and she immediately ducked down and dropped the phone. Feeling around for it, she put it back up to her ear.

"What was that loud noise? Are you okay? What's going on over there?"

"H—hey Ma, I—I gotta go, okay? I love you—bye!" Aris yelled into the receiver before hanging up.

Anytime gunshots rang out meant trouble. She peered over the dashboard and saw another man walking onto the dock with a gun in his hand. "Oh shit, oh shit, oh shit," she mumbled, fumbling to text multiple fire emojis to East's phone. Knowing he likely wasn't in the position to text back, she felt around inside the vehicle for a weapon.

"Come on, come on! There's got to be something in here!" She hissed before opening the glove compartment.

To her surprise, there was nothing there. She

reached underneath the driver's seat and felt around for something—anything she could use to protect herself and him if it came down to it. Her body had gone into full panic mode. If he died, she'd be alone with no protection, and the money he promised her would be nothing but a passing memory.

"Think, Aris! Think!" She said, smashing the palm of her hand against her forehead. Reaching under the seat again, Aris felt underneath her own seat and grabbed a gun from the holster. "Oh, thank God," she squealed.

Without so much as a plan in mind, she quietly exited the car and made her way toward the yacht. The closer she got, she could see East exchanging gunfire with two men. He was outnumbered, and she had to do something to help. Aris snuck onto the boat with the gun in her trembling hand. She didn't know how to shoot, let alone aim, but she was determined to do her best. With her arm extended, she pointed the gun at the back of the other Serbian man's head.

"Move a—and I'll shoot," she whispered, fear clawing at her throat.

The tall man quickly spun around in her direction and charged at her. Aris screamed as his body made contact with hers and pulled the trigger. The two fell back against the railing, and she pushed him off of her. She looked down at her clothes and saw bloodstains as he leaked at her feet. He clawed at his stomach, trying to put pressure on his wound while reaching for his weapon. Aris quickly kicked his gun away from him and grabbed hers again. Instead of shooting him again, she kicked him in his gut to send him flying onto his back.

*****

EAST WAS ENGULFED in rage as his chest rose and fell with rapid breaths. He'd been crouched down behind a fixture trying to figure out his next move with the remaining bullets he had left. He'd been outstripped. It was two against one. All he had to do was wound at least one of them to regain some sort of control over the situation.

"Come out, and let's finish this! It's time to eliminate you completely!" Vlado yelled before firing his weapon in East's direction again.

Catching a glimpse of Vlado's reflection in the glass, East quickly fired his gun, sending two bullets into his arm and chest. Stumbling back, Vlado grabbed hold of the railing before falling to his knees. East fully pulled himself to his feet and wasted no time emptying the remainder of the clip into Vlado's flesh. In the moments passing, everything fell silent. Aris looked around at the carnage around them before turning her eyes to East.

"Oh my God, you're bleeding," she said, pointing right next to his left shoulder.

"It's nothing, it's fine."

"It's not fine! You've been shot! You need medical attention."

"I'm good, Aris. The bullet just grazed me."

She sighed, not understanding how someone could be so difficult after just being shot. "Is there a first-aid kit on board? At least let me clean it and get you patched up."

"Yeah, c'mon, let's go."

Drops of his blood dripped into the sink and on the bathroom tile as she cleaned and dressed his wound. She was grateful to see that his injury wasn't as bad as she first perceived it to be. After he'd been bandaged up, she followed him back out onto the main deck. He bent down to pick up Vlado's phone to finish the wire transfer. The moment the money was in his account, he tossed Vlado's phone overboard. He'd officially become a millionaire and was still able to keep the diamond in his possession.

"Here," he said, handing her the briefcase. "This is yours. You stayed down, Aris. And for that, I'll forever be grateful."

She opened the case, eyes growing wide as she stared at the money he'd promised her inside. "W—wow. I—I don't know what to say."

"I told you I'm a man of my word."

She nodded. "Thank you."

"Smell it. Have you ever smelled anything richer?"

She leaned her face into the bag and drew in a big whiff. Her nose had never known the scent of freshly printed one-hundred-dollar bills before then. She was officially a millionaire, and it was a fantabulous feeling.

"You're free to take the car and go. The plates are clean," he said, his words snapping her back into the moment.

"What about you? Where will you go?"

He lazily shrugged his good shoulder. "Shit, wherever the water takes me."

East's casual tone had made her think about life in an entirely different way. His words made her feel free. She wanted to experience what it felt like to take life by the horns for once instead of fearfully letting it rule her.

"What if I wanted to go with you?"

"You sure about that? If you come with me, your life will never be the same."

"That's what I'm counting on," she told him.

"What made you want to stay?"

"Truth?"

"Always."

"I think I'm in love with the D." She joked.

He chuckled. "Shallow."

"No, I'm joking. To be honest, I've been craving something new, you know? All my life consists of is work and home, work and home. And I know we've only known each other for a blink in time, but you awaken something in me that I've never felt before. It's a crazy, scary, exciting, heart-pounding feeling, and I'm just not ready to get off this rollercoaster yet."

East had blown into her life and turned it upside down as effortlessly as a snow globe, bringing an array of color into her monotonous life. Deep down, she knew there was more to life than an overbearing family and work commitments only growing by the day. She had a little less than a week to figure out what she was going to do about her job or what she'd tell her family and Yara about her whereabouts, but she'd cross that bridge when she got to it.

"It's not going to be easy."

"Nothing has been easy since I met you," she reminded him.

East stared at her blankly while chewing the inside of his lip and running scenario after scenario in his head. The chemistry between them was undeniable, and she'd proven herself to him by holding up her end of the deal. Yet, he'd given her the money, and she still wanted to stay. Being the loner that he was, he knew it was always easier to move solo. He wasn't looking for companionship, let alone love, yet his objections to her coming along with him were approaching zero. Instead of responding with a yes right away, he made his way over to begin lifting the anchor.

Aris then followed him to the boat's steering wheel and watched him type in the GPS coordinates. He pressed the autopilot button and slowly pushed the throttle forward.

"You know how to drive this thing?"

"I took a few lessons a long ass time ago, so I remember enough to get us out of here."

The yacht skimmed over the water, picking up speed as it inched its way further from the dock until they could no longer see land.

"What are we going to do about *them*?" She asked, referring to the two dead bodies they had on board.

"When we get further out to sea, we'll dump them. It won't take long for the sharks to smell the blood in the water."

*****

A FEW STRAY RAYS of sunshine filtered through the curtains, warming the wall across from her. Stretching, she felt his muscular arms slip around her waist as his lips brushed against the nape of her neck. She shivered before slightly turning her head to the side and cracking her eyes open. Bursts of orange, red, and yellow danced through the sky, promising a day of mackerel clouds, crimson and amber-tinted.

She soon felt his fingertips toying with the sides of her panties, inching them down to her ankles. A jolt in her body made her muscles tense and then melt into relaxation. It definitely wasn't how she intended to start her day, but he would hear no complaints from her. East flipped her on her back and dove in between the warmth of her thighs. Drowning in her sea, his tongue danced against her clit.

"Ooooh shit," she squealed, clenching the sheets.

With every moan she made, he could feel the increased blood flow to his dick. East pushed her knees up to her chest and continued to tongue-fucking her into submission. Each stroke making mincemeat of her will.

Aris clenched the silk bedsheets tighter. "You're gonna make me cum if you keep mmm, shit, lickin' me like that," she moaned.

"That's my job," he mumbled, spreading her legs so wide that she wasn't able to clench them.

Her low sultry, incoherent mews only made him more rigid and engorged. He reached down and massaged his erection, keeping his lips fused and held tight against her clit. East slurped her pussy like an ice cream cone melting on a midsummer's day. Aris began circling her hips while bumping her pussy against his long, flat tongue as he massaged her clit.

Her body screamed out in ecstasy. "Ooh shit. Rub it like that! Yeah, rub it like that!" The waves of pleasure were getting stronger. She was seconds away from climaxing. "Ooooh fuckkkkkkkk!"

"That's it, let it fuckin' drip," he said before using his tongue to clean up the sticky mess she'd left behind.

Aris smiled. "Mmm, shit. Well, good morning to you too."

Her morning voice was scratchy as she spoke while rubbing the small remainder of sleep from her eyes.

A ghost of a smile crossed his lips. "Good morning," he replied, tearing himself away from her.

"Where are you going?"

"To make us something to eat. As good as you taste, I'm still hungry."

"Oh," she pouted.

“What?”

“Come back.”

“Tell me what you want.”

Aris crawled off the bed and walked over to him, pressing her naked body against his chest. “I want you to keep making me feel like that,” she whispered against his lips.

His mouth twisted into a smirk. “You need that Vitamin D?”

She nodded. “Yeah, I do.”

“I got you,” he said before fully pressing his lips against hers. Aris stood on the tips of her toes to meet him halfway. They shared a long, liquid kiss that rushed lust through her entire vessel.

They fell back against the bed as his tongue continued to tease her lips apart. His lips began forging a trail down her chest, grazing her nipples with his teeth.

“Mmm,” she moaned. “I know what I want as a belated Christmas gift…”

“What is that?”

“This,” she said, grabbing the imprint of his dick through his boxers.

He flipped over onto his back and propped his head up with his good arm. “Come and get it then.”

Aris wasted no time getting to work when the head of his dick popped out from his shorts. She spit into the palm of her hand before gripping the base, slowly feeding him inside her mouth down as far as she could go before gagging.

"Mmm, yeah, that's it. Get that dick nice and wet," he mumbled.

She flashed her lashes upwards, catching his gaze. He gripped the back of her head, forcing her eyes back down. Aris hollowed her cheeks, letting his length bump the back of her throat.

"Shit, mmm. Choke on that shit, yeah, just like that."

Coming up for air only to smile, Aris swirled her tongue around the head as if his dick was the sweetest thing she'd ever tasted. She whipped her neck forwards and backward while twisting her grip around his dick.

"Goddamn, it feels so good in your fuckin' mouth," he whispered. "You ready for me to put this dick inside you?"

Aris nodded, ready for the one thing she'd been feigning for since he'd broken her back the first time. She crawled from in between his legs and straddled him. East pulled her lips onto his. There was a reckless, savage lust, unlike anything he'd felt before. He *craved* her. Pushing past her walls, his girth stretched her to the brink.

"Ooooh shit," she screamed, sucking air in through her teeth.

East wrapped a hand around her throat, pulling her lips a breath apart from his. Aris could feel the sweat beads forming around her hairline as she glided up and down on his pole. She clenched her muscles as she relentlessly rolled her hips.

"Mmm, grip this dick with that tight ass pussy," he yelled out, clutching her solidly carved thighs and then smacking her ass.

Aris rode him forwards and backward, taking her time on him. They shared a long, slow ride of delight, staring intensely into each other's eyes. East's hands glided down the slope of her back. "Call me Daddy. That's right, call me Daddy," he insisted, taking a handful of her breasts in his grasp.

"Mmm, yes, Daddy!"

He could feel her pussy getting wetter. "Ooooh shit, you fuckin' love that shit, don't you? You like when I talk nasty to you? That's gon' make that pussy cum?"

"Yes! Mmm, fuck! I—I'm about to cum!"

"Mmm, shit, take that dick. Earn your nut!" He commanded.

Aris rode him harder as he thrust upwards, hitting her G-spot. "Ahhhh shit! Shit! Shit! Shit!" She screamed, clamping her eyes shut.

"Yeah, you fuckin' cummin'. I feel you cummin' on this dick. Take that shit til' you mothafuckin' cum!"

"Ahhhhhhhh!" She screamed, relishing in the euphoric state he'd transported her to.

East pulled her onto all fours and guided her hips back against his dick. As soon as he slid inside her, his dick was covered in cream. "That's the shit I like to see," he told her.

He slapped her ass and watched as her hands crumpled the sheets tighter in her grasp. "Yessss!"

"Tell me how you want this dick," he said, each stroke commanding her body to submit to his rule.

"Nice and slow for me, baby."

After a few strokes, Aris began bouncing back against him, matching his rhythm. She could feel his balls slapping against her clit. East firmly pressed his hands into the dimples in her back and picked up the speed. He pressed her face into the pillow as he held her feet in the palms of his hands. "Yeah, take that dick just how I want you to."

Aris could feel her body losing control. He was showing no mercy, and there was nothing she could do about it.

"Ooooh fuck!"

"Over there?"

"Yeah, right there. Oh shit."

"What? Say it louder," he said, running his hand down the curve of her spine.

"Mm, shit. Right there. Don't stop; I'm cumming!"

"I ain't gon' stop. Keep going. Bust some more nuts for Daddy," he commanded.

Aris continued to bounce back against him, even reaching around to spread her cheeks to ensure every inch of him was inside her honey cove.

With her arms draped around his neck, East flipped Aris onto her back without interrupting the stroke. She instantly sank under his body as he loomed over her.

"Oh my God, you feel so fuckin' good!" She screamed, digging her nails into his flesh and leaving claw mark after claw mark.

They both moaned in unison, enjoying the sensuality of it all. He was digging her out and *dicking her down.*

"All of this pussy is yours," she cried.

"It's all mine?" He asked, wrapping his hand around her throat once more.

"Yes!"

"Swear on your life."

"I swear on my life, baby," she said, eyes rolling to the back of her head.

“Look me in the eyes while you cum on this dick,” he demanded, with one of her legs hung over his shoulder.

His eyes hung on the sheer pleasure displayed by her facial expression as he pulled both of her legs over his shoulders. East kneaded his thumbs into the heels of her feet, wanting her to feel pleasure in multiple places at once.

“Mmm, shit! That feels so good,” she panted, her eyes boring into his soul.

East molded himself closer to her, hovering inches from her face and fucking her deeper. “You feel so fuckin’ good,” he praised, lips nuzzled in the crevice of her neck.

“Yes! Yes! Yessss!” She chanted, arching her neck and digging her nails into his back.

East obliged her, giving one final thrust before they both climaxed. The sheets covered the floor as they fell back against the bed, seeing stars. As much as she wanted to bask in the glow of their escapades, she wanted to shower and tame the grumbling in her stomach that she’d been unable to concentrate on until then.

“So about that breakfast?” She asked, turning her neck to him.

“Bet.”

*****

ARIS STEPPED OUT of the shower, wrapped in an oversized soft towel. Instead of getting dressed, she opted to step outside onto the deck with what she had on and let the warm ocean air glide across her skin. She smiled, gazing at the sun's crimson and gold rays spilling light all over the water for miles. Her eyes had never seen a place where the water was so clear she could see through the crest of waves to the clean ocean bottom. Palm trees were swaying on the string of islands in the distance. She wrapped her arms around her body. Soon she'd be laid up on someone's beach with the one person she never knew she needed. When the breakfast he prepared was ready, East walked out to find her standing bare assed with her towel at her feet.

"This is exactly how I wanted to spend my holiday," she admitted as he approached her.

"What? Butt ass naked on a yacht?" He smiled.

Aris gazed out at the varying hues of blue and green. "Yeah," she grinned, "how's your arm feeling?"

He took a sip of his coffee. "It's good, now come eat your breakfast." She smiled and went to bend down to pick up her towel. "Nah, leave it," he told her.

Aris followed him to the table where he had French toast, scrambled eggs, and bacon filling their plates.

"Oh, so you just gon' surprise me with a whole meal?"

"I gets busy in the kitchen. What you know 'bout it?" he asked.

Aris grinned. "Yeah, okay. Well, let's just see what it tastes like," she said, biting into a piece of bacon.

"Yeah, see about it."

Aris scooped some of her scrambled eggs and a corner of a French toast triangle onto her fork and took a bite.

"Well?" He asked.

"So this is what freedom tastes like, huh? If so, I could get used to this." She smiled.

"Welcome to day one of your new life, Aris. Relish in it."

The End

A NOTE FROM K.L. HALL

Reader,

Thank you for reading, *'As Long as You Stay Down.'* Please, if you've made it this far, I hope you'll consider taking a minute to tell me what you thought about the book in the form of a **book review** or **rating**. Don't hesitate to let me know what you'd like to see from me next! I thoroughly enjoy reading your reviews and hearing from you as well! I'm always striving to attract new readers and retain current ones, and reviews are one of the easiest ways to attract readers. If you loved the book, tell a friend, and most importantly, let me know!

All my love,

K.L. Hall

ABOUT THE AUTHOR

As a serial storyteller, K.L. Hall pens enthralling love stories intertwined with the grittiness of urban fiction. Her writing style is a fusion of eminently relatable female characters like Sydney Tate and Raquel Valentine and the flawed yet desirable male leads who love them, like Law Calloway and Justice Silva.

Reader Faves:
In the Arms of a Savage: (Peaked at #1 in Women's Fiction)
A Ruthle$$ Love Story: (Peaked at #3 in Women's Fiction)
Awakened: A Paranormal Romance: (Peaked at #1 in Erotic Science Fiction)

Sign up for my mailing list to stay up to date with new releases, giveaways, sneak peeks, and more! Click this link: https://bit.ly/38RMpV5

Connect with me on social media:

Facebook: K.L. Hall

Twitter: @authorklhall

Instagram: @authorklhall

Website: www.authorklhall.com

Other novels by K.L. Hall:

Diary of a Hood Princess 1-3

Rise of a Street King: The Justice Silva Story *(Spin-Off to the Diary of a Hood Princess series)*

Where He Belongs: A Disrespectful Love Story

Love Me Harder: A Sin City Love Story

Broken Condoms and Promises 1-3

In the Arms of a Savage 1-3

Built for a Savage: Blaze and Camille's Love Story *(Spin-Off to the In the Arms of a Savage Series)*

A Ruthle$$ Love Story 1-3

Fallin' for the Alpha of the Streets 1-2

The Most Savage of Them All: The Wolfe Calloway Story *(Prequel to the In the Arms of a Savage Series)*

When a Gangsta Loves a Good Girl

Caught Between my Husband and a Hustler

Novellas:

Bi-Curious: An Erotic Tale

House of Cards

A Savage Calloway Christmas *(Christmas novella to the In the Arms of a Savage Series)*

Lovin' the Alpha of the Streets: A Valentine's Day Novella *(Valentine's Day novella to the Fallin' for the Alpha of the Streets Series)*

Awakened: A Paranormal Romance

As Long as You Stay Down

Children's Books:

Princess for Hire

Princess Twinkle Toes & the Missing Magic Sneakers

Little One, Change the World

Adjust Your Crown: A Self-Love Coloring Book for Children of Color

www.ingramcontent.com/pod-product-compliance
Lightning Source LLC
LaVergne TN
LVHW010626100826
845148LV00014B/3125

9781736666302